THE UNWRITTEN RULE

Also by Elizabeth Scott

Bloom
Perfect You
Living Dead Girl
Something, Maybe

THE UNWRITTEN RULE

ELIZABETH SCOTT

Simon Pulse

New York   London   Toronto   Sydney

SIMON PULSE
An imprint of Simon & Schuster Children's Publishing Division
1230 Avenue of the Americas, New York, NY 10020
First Simon Pulse hardcover edition April 2010
Copyright © 2010 by Elizabeth Spencer
All rights reserved, including the right
of reproduction in whole or in part in any form.
SIMON PULSE and colophon are registered trademarks
of Simon & Schuster, Inc.
For information about special discounts for bulk purchases,
please contact Simon & Schuster Special Sales at 1-866-506-1949
or business@simonandschuster.com.
The Simon & Schuster Speakers Bureau can bring authors
to your live event. For more information or to book an event contact
the Simon & Schuster Speakers Bureau at 1-866-248-3049 or
visit our website at www.simonspeakers.com.
Designed by Tom Daly
The text of this book was set in Berkeley Book.
Manufactured in the United States of America
2 4 6 8 10 9 7 5 3
Library of Congress Cataloging-in-Publication Data
Scott, Elizabeth, 1972–
The unwritten rule / by Elizabeth Scott. —
p. cm.
Summary: Petite and young-looking, seventeen-year-old
Sarah has been best friends with the glamorous and seductive
Brianna forever, but when she starts liking Brianna's
boyfriend, their friendship becomes precarious.
ISBN 978-1-4169-7891-6 (hardcover)
[1. Best friends—Fiction. 2. Friendship—Fiction. 3. Interpersonal
relations—Fiction. 4. Dating (Social customs)—Fiction.] I. Title.
PZ7.S4195Un 2010
[Fic]—dc22
2009012757

You know whom I want to thank?
You, the person reading this, because if it weren't for readers
like you, this book wouldn't be here.
Thank you!

Thanks to Jen Klonsky, Mara Anastas (who understands my pet peeve!),
Bethany Buck, Paul Crichton, Lucille Rettino, Venessa Williams,
Andrea Kempfer, Lisa Fyfe, Jessica Handelman, Emilia Rhodes,
Michelle Fadlalla, Charlie Young—in short, everyone at Simon Pulse.
Thanks for all you do and for your belief in me—
you all make writing a joy!

Thanks also go to the usual suspects: Robin Rue, Beth Miller,
Diana Fox, Shana Jones, Katharine Beutner, Clara Jaeckel,
Amy Pascale, and Jessica Brearton.

Finally, I want to thank a few people from my mailing list—
proof that I have the BEST fans around: Brittney Tabel,
Emily Cassady, Amber White, Karly Hemshrot, Ashley Evans,
Alexa Patton, Kat Werner, Samantha Marie, Michelle Andreani,
Renee Combs, Jessica Launius, Brittani Zarate, Dominique McCaig,
Shalonda Dixon, Caroline Dougherty, and Lucy Dason.

THE UNWRITTEN RULE

one

I liked him first, but it doesn't matter.

I still like him.

That doesn't matter either.

Or at least, it's not supposed to.

two

Brianna and Ryan are kissing. I try not to notice, but when you're the only person in the room who isn't wrapped around someone else, it's kind of hard not to. Also, the movie Brianna has picked is one I've seen before.

More than once.

Thirty-seven times, to be exact.

I know it's a lot, but Brianna really likes it, and it's better than what's on at my house, which is either the news or old sitcoms—Dad's favorites—or DVDs Mom's made from footage of her in different cooking contests. Since she entered the Fabulous Family Cook-Off, she's been "studying" herself at other cook-offs to see how she can "improve her prep work."

Yes, I have watched my mother watch herself chopping onions. And then watched her critique herself on it.

So you can see why I'd rather watch a movie and why, as of right now, I'm on viewing thirty-seven of "girl meets boy, girl falls for boy, boy falls for girl, then boy gets cancer and dies while girl is brave and only cries once, at the end, as the boy says, 'I'll wait for you,' and then dies."

I admit, I cried the first time I saw it. And the second. But by the third time, I started to wonder about the girl's best friend, who shows up at periodic intervals throughout the movie to support the girl, usually by providing ice cream and/or doing something stupid-silly like catching her skirt in the door and tugging until she tears herself out of it. She also sings to an umbrella at one point.

Anyway, by the third time through, I started wondering about the best friend. How come she has to be klutzy and wacky? Doesn't she get tired of being supportive and eating ice cream? (Well, maybe not so much on the last thing.)

What's the best friend's life *really* like? She must do something when she isn't losing her skirt or saying, "Oh, you're so brave!"

So far, the best friend has been the following—at least in my mind:

—a secret heroin user (that was the week Ryan took Brianna to the awesome indie film about the model who stayed skinny by shooting heroin and how everyone told her how fabulous she looked right up until she died. I ended up going with them because Brianna said she wanted someone to talk to when she got bored. So I listened to her guess who was going to win the new date-a-rockstar reality show episode where all the girls have to try to fry an egg naked without burning themselves. But what I saw of the movie was great, and I went back and saw it with my mother later. She said it was "depressing," but at least I got to see the whole thing.)

—a spy (because hi, obvious awesome plot!)

—a superhero who is trying to save the world while keeping her disguise as a mild-mannered klutz (another obvious but awesome plot)

—in love with the boy, who loves her back, and they have secret meetings—when the girl is in one of her musical montages—and the boy tells the best friend he really wants her, but doesn't want to hurt the girl, and the best friend agrees because she's really a good person in spite of the fact that she's totally into her best friend's boyfriend.

That last one is—well, I try not to think about it, but I do.

I do because I can see it happening—in the movie, I mean—and the best friend is a nice person. Really, she is. She can't help the way she feels about the guy.

She really can't. Trust me on this one. I might be . . .

Oh, forget it. I am. I'm that girl. The one who likes her best friend's boyfriend. In the world of friendship, I'm awful. Everyone knows the unwritten rule: You don't like your best friend's boyfriend.

I know that, I do, and I don't want to like Ryan. He's Brianna's boyfriend. She's crazy about him. If I turned my head a little, I could see them kissing. I know they're together. I know it's BriannaandRyan now.

I don't look at them. I don't need the reminder that they're together.

And besides, I know that if I look it'll hurt too much.

So I watch the movie. Maybe the best friend is secretly an assassin from the future, and has come back through time to make sure an evil scientist is stopped before he destroys mankind.

A sofa throw pillow hits me in the head, and since I know who did it, I say, "Hey, Brianna, what if I miss what's going to happen next?"

Brianna laughs and I make myself look back at her.

She grins at me, lips not attached to Ryan any longer. "So, are you coming with us tonight or what?"

I pretend to stretch so I can look at the clock. It's only ten. Too early to say I have to go home. I'll have to make up a reason why I can't go with her. Them.

"I can't. Mom wants me to get up at five tomorrow and go shopping with her. She's doing another test run of her recipes in case she gets the call."

"Why do you have to go?" Brianna says.

"My dad can't because of his hip, and she wants someone there to help."

This is a lie. My mother doesn't need help when she's grocery shopping. She knows every grocery store in a fifty-mile radius like she knows our house. She knows who gets produce in when, which stores get the newest products first, and which ones are open late in case inspiration strikes and she wants to make something at 10 p.m.

Mom is intensely, fiercely focused on creating recipes. She

enters cooking contests all the time, and has "placed" in four, which is cook-off lingo for coming in second or third—which everyone, even Mom, says they're happy about, but isn't.

Mom wants to win a cook-off. I know she does. She likes cooking, she likes making up recipes, but she also enters seemingly every single cook-off there is. She keeps it pretty low-key—especially compared to some of the other "contesters" I've met—but it's there and it drives her to keep going.

She's always had that drive, I think. I mean, there's a reason I quickly learned to play Go Fish with Dad and not her when I was little—with Dad, I at least won sometimes.

This year she's sent in—and is now practicing—twenty recipes for the Fabulous Family Cook-Off. This is a low number in the contesting world, at least among the diehards, but Mom decided the key was to really focus on "just a few dishes." Dad and I have been eating them for a while now because she wants to be ready when (my mother doesn't believe in "if" when it comes to cook-offs) she gets the call.

Unfortunately, Brianna knows all of this, and that's the problem with having a best friend who's known you since you were five. Twelve years of friendship mean Brianna knows almost everything about me and my family.

"She doesn't need you to go," Brianna says. "She knows where everything is in every grocery store around here, and besides, she's never needed your help shopping before. She has a system and everything." (Brianna's right, Mom does. She can find anything in any store in a minute, tops, and probably blindfolded to boot.)

But, of course, this doesn't help with the excuse thing at all.

"Maybe Sarah doesn't want to go to the party," Ryan says, looking at the framed photo of Brianna that Brianna's hung on the far wall. I took it last year, when I signed up for Photography thinking it would be an easy A.

It was a very hard B-, with a lot of bad photos on my part, but the picture of Brianna is a good one. She's sitting on her front steps, looking off into the distance, and I'd messed with the timer and the speed so much that I accidentally managed to get myself in the shot as I was running back to the camera to see if it was still working. I turned out as a smudge, a sort of blur of motion, but Brianna is perfectly still, perfectly captured. I messed around with the photo a little and got Brianna to almost glow in it, pushed the blur that was me into a ghostly shimmer.

"She wants to go," Brianna says to Ryan, and then nudges me with a foot. "I hear Tommy might be there."

I shrug. Tommy is in my English and Chemistry classes, and he's sweet. He's also hopelessly in love with Brianna.

However, unlike most of the guys who are hopelessly in love with Brianna, he knows he has no chance with her. So he has decided he likes me. Today, in school, he asked me if I was going to be at the party tonight, and I watched him start to ask if Brianna was coming too and then stop, remember she has a boyfriend.

I watched him remember he was supposed to like me.

"You don't think he's cute?" Brianna says.

"He's okay." He is. He's okay. He has eyes and a nose and a mouth and hair that doesn't look like it was cut by a lawn mower and his clothes aren't hideous and he doesn't smell or spit when he talks.

"So, come with us. There's always room in Ryan's car, you know. The whole school could fit in his car. Which is fine! Great!" She rolls her eyes at me.

I smile, because there is always room in Ryan's car. He drives a station wagon, and Brianna hates it. She wants Ryan to ask his parents for a new car, and has since they started going out a little over six weeks ago.

"I like my car," Ryan says, and glances at me.

I let myself look at him for just a second, get a glimpse of dark hair, bright, intense eyes (so blue you'd swear they came straight from the sky on a hot summer day, the kind of day where even the clouds have burned away), and the tiny scar that cuts across the corner of his right eyebrow that he got during a soccer match back in seventh grade.

"I can't go," I say. "I mean, I can, but I'm tired and I had to eat Cheesy Corn and Rice Casserole for dinner again and my stomach hurts—I mean, it's the fourth night in a row I've had to eat it—so I'd rather just go home and—"

"Pleeeeeeease," Brianna says.

"I'm too full of corn and rice to be any fun."

"You're full of something all right," she says, shaking her head, and then sighs. "Fine. Go home, leave me and Ryan all by ourselves at the party."

"You'll have fun," I say.

"I know," she says. "I just like it if you're there. I always like it if you're there."

I look at Ryan again, one last quick glance before I go.

He's looking at me, and for a second, one crazy second before I stand up and smile and say goodbye and good night and walk out to my car, I think about what it would be like to be the one sitting next to him.

three

I've liked Ryan for a long time. An embarrassingly long time, but nobody, not even Brianna, knows that. She thinks that back in eighth grade, when he asked me to a dance and I said yes, I was just being nice, and when I said, "I . . . I sort of like him, okay?" hoping she'd say it was, she said, "Come on, you can't really like him. He's *Ryan*."

I can still remember her telling me how lucky I was when it turned out he couldn't go because his grandma died and he had to fly to Seattle for the funeral. Back then Ryan wasn't worth Brianna's time or notice, and so he wasn't supposed to be worth mine.

But I thought he was. I wanted to go to that dance with him, I wanted to be his girlfriend, but we didn't get to go to the dance, and when he came back from the funeral Brianna had told everyone I hadn't wanted to go with Ryan and was just too nice to say no.

He heard, of course, and we didn't really talk again until the end of our freshman year, when we ended up standing next to each other during the wait to leave school during a fire drill. (I can't be the only person who sees the problems with that, can I?)

We talked that day—just "Hey, what's going on?" and guessing how burnt we'd be if there was an actual fire—and after that, I admit, I thought—hoped, that maybe, one day . . .

And then, a little over six weeks ago, I saw him at a party.

I saw him, but Brianna got him.

I see Brianna waving as I pull onto the road. Ryan raises one hand too, and I try not to think about that party. About what I'd thought then.

About his hand touching mine.

four

The party where Brianna and Ryan got together was an end-of-summer-oh-crap-school-is-going-to-suck thing, and all the usual suspects were there. Brianna ran into a bunch of people from drama club, and they were all talking about what play they wanted to do. I was looking around the house, saying hi to everyone I passed and talking about summer, which we all agreed was too short.

I got sidetracked in the study, which was your usual study—a dad refuge complete with comfy, dumpy chair that clearly wasn't allowed in any other room in the house, a collection of newspapers and magazines all opened to articles about sports, and two huge bookshelves. They ran from floor to ceiling and were filled with paperbacks and what looked like old textbooks, but there were also some coffee table books, the kind that are all pictures. One of them was about shoes.

And here's the thing about me: I like shoes. Well, sneakers. I have twenty-seven pairs, and twenty-five of them are ones I either decorated myself or bought custom-designed. (Two pairs are in my room now, plain white and waiting for inspiration to strike.)

Which leads me to what happened. There I was, thumbing through the shoe book and wondering if I could get a copy and decorate a pair of sneakers with pictures of shoes (I saw heels running around the edges, boots dancing along the top, and bright yellow laces with tiny silver shoe charms at the ends), when I saw a painting on the wall.

I don't know a lot about art, but the painting was clearly valuable. It was nicely framed and had one of those little "Look! Look at this ART!" spotlights above it. I half expected to see one of those little white cards bolted to the wall next to it with a title like *Internal Struggle of the Human Spirit (Season 8)* but there wasn't anything there, just the painting and its light.

And the painting . . . well, it looked like crap.

I don't mean that figuratively, I mean it literally.

I moved a little closer, interested and horrified, and practically had my nose up against the glass frame when someone else came into the room. I looked over, saw it was Ryan, and grinned at him.

And then I felt my heart drop into my stomach because—

Well, the summer had been really, REALLY good to him.

Ryan had always been three things: short, skinny, and obsessed with art. But over the summer, he'd grown—I had to look up in order to meet his eyes—and although he was still thin, he wasn't skinny. He had muscles. Not the big, bulky kind you think of whenever you hear the word, but long, lean ones.

He looked—oh, I wish I was a poet—but he looked beautiful in this raw, exotic way, and when he said, "Hey, Sarah," I wanted to run over to him and trace the high lines of his cheekbones with my fingers and then touch his hair.

And all right, the rest of him.

I didn't, though. I just said, "Hey, Ryan, come tell me what this is," like he was still regular old Ryan, the one who'd thrown up before giving an oral report in fifth grade—and not this suddenly gorgeous creature whose face, which had been all angles and huge, startling blue eyes, had suddenly come together in a way that worked and sent me reeling.

"Well, it's a painting," he said, grinning at me. I'd always liked Ryan's smile—it was friendly and warm—but now, in that face that had come into itself, it was lethal.

"I—uh. I sort of figured out that one," I said, clearing my throat and trying to talk normally.

I knew from Brianna that being beautiful wasn't all great. Brianna had changed in middle school. One day we were both seventh graders and the next, she was a supermodel who had a seventh grader for a best friend.

Maybe it wasn't that dramatic, but it was still pretty sudden.

Brianna had always been pretty, but she got beautiful fast, and people noticed. She liked it at first, until it was all they noticed. And then she got used to it. Still, that took a while, and I remember her screaming, "I'm more than breasts, you know!" to a guy we met at the mall right after it all changed for her, and how she'd cried that night in my room, hating that people looked at her and saw her body and face and nothing more.

"It looks like . . ." Ryan said, and then trailed off, squinting at the painting.

"Crap?" I said, and he grinned at me again. My stomach flipped from that smile—from him—and I swallowed hard. I told myself it was Ryan, and that I'd known and liked him forever.

The thing was, I'd *liked* him forever.

"It does, but I don't think it is," he said, and he still sounded the same, still sounded like Ryan, with a voice that had always been a little too serious and deep for him before.

It fit now.

"I think it's dirt," he said, and pointed at the painting, careful not to touch the glass. "Look, see this?"

I looked, and saw only his reflection in the glass.

I nodded anyway.

"It looks like a smudged handprint," he said. "Like someone left a mark, and time and nature have worn it away. Maybe it's about what's left after you create something. The bits you aren't supposed to see but that have to be for a painting to exist."

Now he really sounded like the Ryan I knew, the one I'd waved at in the halls every day last year, the one who was my friend.

"Or some guy just thought, hey, I have this brown goop, why don't I smear some on a canvas?" I said.

"Cynic," he said, grinning wider. "Where have you been all summer, anyway?"

"Me?" I am embarrassed to report that I squeaked. Like, an actual squeak.

"Yeah, I didn't see you around."

"That's because I was home, helping out and stuff. My dad paid me to paint the garage."

Great. Now I sounded like a fourth grader. My dad paid me to paint the garage! I have no life!

"I painted too," he said. "Houses, I mean. Not painting painting. I mean, I did some of that, but mostly it was houses. Which I already said."

I relaxed a little more then. In spite of how he looked, he really was still Ryan.

"So that's how you got all those muscles," I said, and poked his arm. He shrugged, blushing a little.

Imagine a guy. He's a little taller than you, with perfect skin, skin that just screams "touch me!" and dark hair and gorgeous blue eyes and he looks so sweet and he is sweet. And then have him blush a little.

Surely you can understand why I dropped the book I was still holding.

He bent down to get it when I did, and for a moment we were so close I could have leaned over and kissed him.

"Here," he said, handing the book to me. We were still so

close, and he was looking at me, the smile in his eyes darkening into something deeper, more intense.

"Thanks," I said, although I'm betting it sounded more like "Geratyuhrh," and then I reached for the book and he gave it to me, his hands touching mine for a moment.

And then he said, "Sarah," and touched my hand again. I looked down. My fingers were spotted with the dark green my father had wanted the garage painted, and his hands were spotted too, white and yellow, and the book slid to the floor as he did more than touch my hand. He held it, he slid his fingers into mine.

Our palms pressed together, and all I could think of was a line I'd read somewhere, about palms pressed together like a kiss, and he was still looking at me and then we were standing up, still holding hands, and he was close, so close and he was leaning in and I couldn't breathe, couldn't move, could only watch and wait, hoping and breathless as he moved close and closer and—

"Sarah, you will not believe what I just heard the fall play is going to be. It's—oh," Brianna said, and stopped talking.

Looked right at Ryan, and smiled the smile she did when she saw a guy she wanted to see.

"Hi there," she said, and she was gorgeous, tan and tall and beautiful, her black hair curling around her heart-shaped face, and I saw Ryan smile back.

"Hey, Brianna," he said, and she said, "What have you been doing all summer? Come tell me everything while I go to the store for some soda." She grinned at me. "I have to get away for a little bit. One more story about acting camp and I'll start screaming, I swear. I wish I could have gone."

"I know," I said, because I'd been there when her mother told her no, and tried not to notice that my hand wasn't touching Ryan's anymore. "Don't just get grape soda, okay?"

"I wouldn't get just grape—well, all right, I would. But I won't," she said, and looped her arm through Ryan's, steering him out of the room. Steering him to her like only she could do, and by the time he and Brianna came back with a few six-packs of soda, both of their mouths were slightly purple. Brianna grinned at me, a pleased, glowing smile, and said, "Ryan likes grape soda too," as she tossed me a root beer and said, "Here's your favorite."

"Mine too, actually," Ryan said, but he wasn't looking at me as he did. He was looking at Brianna, a little bewildered, a little dazed, and I knew he wasn't going to turn away.

I looked at her, and she was smiling the smile she wore when she saw a guy she wanted, and that's when I knew she'd get him because that's who she was and what she did.

I saw she already had him.

I went into the kitchen to drink my root beer. I poured it in a glass, added ice, and then waited for the fizz to settle. Delaying tactics, and by the time I drank it and went back to where Brianna was, she and Ryan were sitting together, talking.

Brianna was nodding intently, like everything he was saying meant the world to her. Ryan still looked slightly dazed but saw me and started to say something, and then Brianna touched his face and kissed him in front of everyone.

And that was it. He was hers.

He might have talked to me first. He even held my hand first. But it didn't matter.

Except to me.

five

I take the long way home because I don't want to be thinking about Ryan and Brianna when I get there. I don't want to play "what if" like I'm more than half doing already. I want to be happy for Brianna and nothing more.

But when I get home, Ryan's car is in the driveway.

I pull up alongside it, my stomach twisting even as my heart (stupid, traitorous) flutters in my chest, making me dizzy.

I look at my porch and see my dad and Brianna and Ryan sitting there, the three of them partially lit by the big frosted globe Mom won as a second-place finalist in the Best Houses and Lifestyle Magazine Super Porch Suppers! Competition. (She did mini–meatloaves with a honey-mustard glaze and serrano chili corn muffins with honey butter. Number of times I ate that for dinner: about sixty. It was fine—the first forty times. The last twenty were pretty tough, but Mom likes to know her recipes inside and out.)

I look at Ryan and Brianna—I make myself see them—and my heart stops fluttering because this is how things are. This is reality.

But why are they here?

"Hi, Sarah Bear," Dad says, standing up and hugging me like I'm six and not seventeen. I sigh but hug him back, glad he isn't wincing from his bad hip.

"Why are you on the porch?" I ask him, and then look at Brianna. "And how did you get here before me?"

Brianna rolls her eyes at me. "You drive like an old man, Sarah." She glances at my dad. "No offense, Mr. F."

"None taken," he says, and ruffles her hair. I hate it when he does it to me, because it reminds me that my hair is not glossy and perfect-looking, but instead pretty much looks like someone's ruffled it all the time. Brianna likes it, though—she always has—and shoots him a shy smile before turning to Ryan and looping an arm around his shoulders.

"Anyway," she says. "We're here to kidnap you. It's Friday night and my best friend can't be sitting home alone. I mean, you do that all the time already!"

I try not to wince at that but do—Brianna's right, but still, it hurts—and then Dad adds, "Sarah Bear, you don't have to be home until one, you know. And besides, there's no need to hang around the house tonight." He grins at me. "Not unless you want to listen to my lecture on jurisprudence. Or remind me to take my arthritis pills, which your mother has already done twice even after I told her I took them."

My dad is old for a dad—he was fifty when I was born—and he retired from practicing law seven years ago and now teaches part-time at Crestwood University. He likes it a lot, but I know he misses being a lawyer. He has rheumatoid arthritis, which means his immune system attacks his joints, or, as he's always reminding me, the joint tissues. (I don't see the distinction. All I know is that it's awful and it hurts him.) It ended up getting so bad that he couldn't work full-time anymore, and so he had to stop.

I know what Mom asking about his pills means and look at him. "How's your hip?"

"Still attached to the rest of me," he says with a grin, and I look down at the sneakers I'm wearing because I know he's in pain and I wish there was something I could do for it. For him. But I can't.

The sneakers I'm wearing are one of my favorite pairs: bright pink, with the lining and the tongue done in a black-and-white skull print, black stitching and soles, and bright pink laces.

Seeing them doesn't make me feel better.

The thing about Dad leaving the law firm all those years ago was that it meant his arthritis had gone from being an on-and-off thing—sometimes he had horrible attacks, and then they would let up and he'd feel okay—to pretty much constant pain. His hip actually got dislocated by it last year, and although that was fixed, his hip bone is still eroding.

I don't like thinking about that much. It's scary to think of your bones being eaten away by your own body. It's scary to think about how sick Dad is—and how much worse he could get.

I don't want that to happen. I like having him and Mom home all the time. Around all the time. Mom's actually been home since I can remember—she has a doctorate in medieval history, but gave up trying to find a job after two post-doctoral positions never went anywhere, and discovered cooking and then contesting.

Basically, I spend a lot of time with my parents, but the thing is . . . I like it. I like them. I wouldn't trade my parents for anything, and so I worry about Dad, whose arthritis isn't getting better—or even staying the same—despite his pills. He's gone from walking five miles every day to three or fewer. On really bad days, he doesn't walk at all.

"So," Brianna says, waving a hand in front of my eyes, "like I said, we're kidnapping you. Ryan, quick, grab her and let's go!"

I move then, getting up so Ryan won't feel like he has to touch me. I try not to look at him as I do, but can't help myself and see that he is looking at me.

I swallow and Dad laughs, says, "Sarah Bear, I don't think Ryan would hurt you. In fact, I'm not sure he could pick you up."

"Thanks, Dad," I say, and he shakes his head and says, "Oh, no, no, I didn't mean—well, you're tiny, Sarah Bear. You know that. I meant Ryan isn't very big—not that you aren't capable, I'm sure, Ryan. But you don't seem the type to run around grabbing—" He clears his throat. "Well. Why don't I go inside and see if your mother needs any help?"

"Dad," I say, half embarrassed, half worried about him, but

when I go to open the door for him, he shakes his head at me and says, "Go on, have fun."

"Make sure you take those pills," Brianna says, and my father smiles, says, "I'm going to put a note on my forehead that says, 'Yes, I really did take my medicine,'" and ruffles her hair again before he goes inside.

"He's adorable," Brianna says, and grabs my hand. "Now come on, Sarah Bear, and get your shrimpy ass in gear."

"I'm not shrimpy," I say, sighing as Brianna tugs me down the steps to Ryan's car. "I'm . . . small-boned."

By which I mean I have no chest, no ass, and the overall body of a twelve-year-old girl, right down to the fact that I barely clear five foot two. Which would be fine if I was twelve. But is not so fine when you are seventeen and your best friend has the kind of body that makes guys do things like stop and stare even if they are with another girl.

"You're petite," Ryan says from behind me, and Brianna says, "Which is why you should get a new car. I mean, Sarah takes up no room at all." She grins at me as I slide into the back seat. "Look, she's practically lost back there. A new, smaller car would be way more comfortable for her."

"Yes, Captain Tiny is adrift back here," I say as I buckle my seatbelt.

"What, no more Girl Overboard?" Ryan says, his grin flashing before he slides into the front seat, and I know he's thinking about the class trip we took last year, when we both got seasick and spent the ride out—and back—leaning over the rail in shared misery.

I blush, pleased and scared.

"You two are weird," Brianna says. "But I still like you."

"Thanks," Ryan and I say at the same time, and Brianna laughs and starts kissing Ryan's neck.

I rest my hands on my knees and look at them, watch the little glimpses of knuckle that appear every time we drive under a streetlight.

"Okay, fine, pull away from me," Brianna says after a moment.

"I'm not—I'm driving," Ryan says.

"You can't take a second and kiss me?"

"No. I mean, I—I am driving and this car is, you know."

I stare harder at my hands. As much as I don't like being around Ryan and Brianna when they are kissing, this is even worse. And the reality is that these tense moments are a lot more common than the kissing, and have been for a while now.

"Okay, so you're driving," Brianna says, and I hear how hard she's trying to sound happy. "Will you at least think about asking for a better one?"

"I like my car."

"It's not you."

"It is me."

"Sarah doesn't even have a car, so a car can't be who you are," Brianna says. "Right, Sarah?"

"I—well, I'm supposed to be getting my mom's at some point," I say, the tension I feel—and that's in the car—eating my insides. "But then that would make me bright orange and dented. So I don't know."

Brianna glances at me briefly, and I can tell she's upset I didn't agree with her. I lean forward to try and do something, say something, but she looks away and turns on some music.

She finds a song she likes and turns it up loud, so loud the car windows are practically vibrating. So loud there's no way anyone can say anything.

six

The party is in someone's basement, one of those
hey-we-did-this-for-you-kid-so-don't-mess-up-the-house thing. It's
got every gadget you could want, but of course no one's bothering
with them because everyone is too busy dancing or messing around
with the croquet set that someone's found and set up.

Brianna heads straight for the dancing, and Ryan and I end up
playing croquet for a while. I make sure I'm not standing near him,
because—well—because.

Tommy comes over to me as I've finished what feels like my
millionth turn and am waiting to go again.

"Hey," he says. "Look at you."

"Hey, Tommy," I say, and watch him smile at me. He really is okay looking, and he smells—well, he smells like aftershave.

My *dad's* aftershave.

"You look great," he says, only just glancing at Brianna as he says it, and I have to say, while it's creepy to be complimented by a guy who smells like my father, I actually feel sort of bad for Tommy. Brianna was into him for about a week last year, and then she decided she wasn't and moved on.

He didn't. Most of Brianna's guys don't. I mean, they don't trail after her in school or anything, but you just know, even when they're with someone else, that if she was interested again they'd come running back. She's got this way of making it so the guy wants her more than she wants him, so the guy wants her forever and is left thinking of her even when she's gone on to someone else.

"So, you wanna sit down or something?" Tommy says, and I shrug, dropping my mallet, and we go sit on the lawn chairs that have been put in a semi-circle around the edge of the croquet set-up. At first he's all nervous, but then I ask him about his band, which I remember Brianna complaining about, and pretty soon he's off and running.

I like music, although I'm not sure *Tommy's Banana Brain Pain* necessarily qualifies as it. I do like the name, though. He tells me he'll get me a T-shirt when I say that, and then goes on to tell me about their ironic cover of some boy band song that I remember loving when I was in first grade.

"So, how's Brianna doing?" he says, and I look at him trying not to look at her. Poor guy.

"She's good," I say, and nudge Tommy with my elbow. "She always liked your band."

"Really?"

I nod and he smiles at that, wider and happier than I've seen him smile the whole time he's been with me. I look around the room and spot Laura Kirst looking at him.

"You know who else likes your band a lot?" I say. "Laura."

"She does?"

"Yep. You know, you should go tell her about that song thing," I say. "She'll love it." She will. Laura only wears T-shirts from the 1990s, and if anyone would love hearing about an ironic boy band cover, it's her.

Plus it's obvious she thinks Tommy is cute.

"Nah," Tommy says, but he's looking at Laura now, and she gives him a shy grin. I see him glance at me, and then grin back at her.

"Hey, I'm going to get a drink," I say. "See you around?"

"Yeah," he says, and as I'm looking for a root beer—and having to settle for a Coke—I see him sit down next to her. She looks really happy and he isn't even glancing at Brianna. (Well, once, but just for a second.)

"So, Tommy and Laura?" Ryan says, and I look over at him, startled.

"Looks like it," I say, and take a big sip of Coke to make myself stop looking at him. "Provided she likes hearing about his band."

"I thought he liked you."

I force a laugh. "No, he just liked talking about . . . we just talk sometimes."

"You always find girls for guys who still like Brianna?"

I glance at him to see if he looks jealous or angry about Tommy still being into Brianna. He doesn't sound like it, and he doesn't look upset at all. He's smiling.

And looking at me.

"I don't . . ." I say, and then trail off, because he's raised the eyebrow with the scar and I just . . . I just want to lean into him. Right now, right here, in front of everyone. In front of my best friend.

"You should go dance with Brianna," I say, and move a little bit away from him, wrapping my now shaking hands tightly around my soda.

"I don't really dance like she does. You know that."

"Who can?" I say, ignoring the last part of what he said because I have to. I can't think about him dancing. I just can't. The mention of that boat ride last year was enough to get me wishing and—

Nope. Not doing that.

I look at Brianna swaying her hips, grinning at me as she flips her hair back and does a shimmy hip swivel thing that I could practice in my room for a thousand hours and still never master, and add, "And besides, Brianna won't care. She likes you, she likes everything about you."

"Except my car," he says.

"Okay, except that."

"And my hair."

I laugh, sure he's kidding, but he doesn't laugh too, and so I turn it into a sort of cough and take another sip of my soda.

"What's wrong with your hair?" I know I should drag him out to Brianna and watch her sway her arms around him, but that's what comes out instead. And she can't really not like his hair. Can she?

"She says it's too long," he says, running a hand through it, and I watch it fall back down over his forehead, the ends of it trailing down around his eyes, soft dark waves that I would love to touch.

"Oh," I say, because I can't touch his hair or say I think it looks great because I am her best friend and he is her boyfriend. I don't know why Brianna asked me to come over to her house and watch that movie with them or wanted me at this party, but I do know I want to go home and not think about how much I wish Ryan and I were standing here talking for real instead of talking about him and Brianna.

"I'm pretty tired," I say. "I should probably go." I manage to fake a credible yawn and turn away to toss my soda.

"Hold on, I'll go tell Brianna," he says, and crap, I came with them. I should have just said I had to go talk to someone and found a ride home with them. I don't want to leave with Brianna and Ryan, I don't want to sit in the car with them, I don't want to see *them*—

"Sarah, you want to leave?" Brianna says, coming up behind me and flinging her arms around me. Even sweating, she still looks gorgeous. "How come?"

I can't say, "Because I want to fling myself at your boyfriend and also, it's exhausting to want him and feel guilty for it at the same time," so I just say, "Tired. Sorry, I suck."

"Just hang out with us for a while longer, okay?"

There's something in her voice and I glance at her, but she's turned her face away and is looking back out at everyone dancing.

"I can't, I gotta find someone and get a ride, but call me tomorrow," I say, and bump my hip against hers.

"I'll take you home," Ryan says, and I glance at him, surprised. He's got his hands shoved in his pockets, his face a little flushed, and Brianna says, "Yeah, go with Ryan, okay?" and then gives me a hug.

"Ask him why he won't hang out with me," she whispers as she puts her arms around me. "He doesn't even care that I'm dancing with guys who I used to go out with, and at first the no-jealousy thing was cool, but now it's . . . I don't know. Also, tell him to get his hair cut."

She heads back into the group of people who are dancing, turning to wave at Ryan before she sways toward one of her exes, Greg, who looks very happy to see her.

I turn toward Ryan, ready to tell him that he doesn't need to worry about me, that I'll be able to find a ride home and he should go hang out with Brianna, but he's not even looking at her. She's right, he's not jealous. That's never happened before.

"Ready to go?" he says, and I nod, confused and some . . . other things. Things that I shouldn't be feeling. But that I do anyway.

seven

"You really don't have to drive me home," I say when we're outside.

"My car's that bad?" he says, glancing at me, and I start to say "no" and then see he's grinning.

"It's hideous," I tell him as I get in. "For starters, it's not orange like the one I've been promised for so long I'm pretty sure I'm never going to actually get it, and for another, where are the dents? How can you not drive a car that has dents from where your mother got distracted thinking about tortillas and bean pizza sauce?"

"Bean pizza sauce?"

"Yep," I say. "After Mom scraped the side up in the grocery store parking lot, she wrote down her recipe for Mexican Tortilla

Pizza. See, all contest recipes have a twist. Or at least the winning ones do, according to my mother. And she does know a lot about cook-offs. And cooking too, but the cook-off thing is—well, you know. Her thing."

"She's made some amazing stuff. I still remember those turtle cookies she made for your eighth birthday."

"It's hard to forget things like someone's mother setting up a river of chocolate sauce and then making everyone wait to eat while she set up the turtles in their 'home,'" I say. "Worst. Birthday. Party. Ever."

"No way," he says. "It was cute."

"Making people wait to eat cookies and then saying there's no cake isn't cute. I think people actually took their gifts back before they left."

"Well, I can top that. I had to get braces on my tenth birthday."

"You didn't!"

He nods. "I did. Oh, hey, my sketchbook is headed your way." We turn a corner and it slides off the dashboard and into my lap.

"You drive and draw?" I say, waving a finger at him—it feels so great to be like this, to talk, and I'm flirting, I know, but it's just a little.

He grins, his teeth flashing as we drive down the dark streets that lead to my house. "I'm trying to get some dents and improve the car's look."

I laugh and tap the sketchbook. "Are you still doing those pencil drawings like last year?"

"You remember those?" he says, sounding surprised, and glances at me.

I do, and wonder if I shouldn't still know that he had a bunch of his drawings displayed at an exhibit at Dad's college last year. I saw them and told him I liked them when we both ended up standing in line for lunch at the same time, but that was last year, and as a non-interested-in-him person, am I allowed to remember that?

I doubt it.

I put the sketchbook back on the dashboard and say, "You had some drawings in a thing at the college, right? Dad's always dragging me and Mom there to look at stuff."

"Yeah," he says. "That was me. You probably don't remember, but you told me you liked them last year, and I thought—well, it was really nice of you."

He does remember!

I knit my fingers together to try and keep them from shaking. It doesn't work very well. "So, are you still doing stuff like that?"

"Yeah," he says. "I just did this series of hands. I found all these photos of my grandparents—my grandmother played the piano and my grandfather played the violin, and their hands when they're playing—it's amazing. Just . . . it's like they're talking with them, like I can hear the music and I want to try and show that." He clears his throat. "Sorry, I know it's boring."

I shake my head. "It's not. I wish I could draw, but a straight line is beyond me."

"What about those cubes you do in class?" he says, and I look over at him, surprised—and happy—that he's noticed what I do in class. Especially since we don't even have any together this term.

"Okay, I can draw cubes," I say. "Maybe I should quit school. I could travel around the world drawing cubes on things like bridges or banks. My parents can use my college money for bail. They'd love that."

He grins again and says, "Maybe you can get your start at home. Cube up your front porch or something."

"Wait, we're here?" I say, and then quickly add, "I mean, thanks for bringing me home."

"It was fun," Ryan says, which is a nice thing to say, a him thing to say, but when I look at him, one more look before he goes back to the party, to my best friend, he's looking at me like—

Well, like he *wants* to look at me. Like he likes what he sees, and he's smiling and his eyes are so blue, even in the faint glow of the porch light they shine, and I nod dumbly, blindly, and then grope for the door handle, telling myself to look away and yet not able to do it.

"Sarah," he says, softly, almost hesitantly, and my heart slam-bangs, beating hard, and this is what it's like to want someone you can't have. To want someone you shouldn't even be looking at.

It's wrong, so wrong, to be here, but longing is eating away at my insides till it's all I am, till I'm a quivering husk swaying toward him. I hear the slow, soft hiss of my seatbelt as it stretches, the faint echo to the pounding of my heart beating in my fingers and my toes, a roaring in my ears, and he is so close, and then closer still, flicker flash of his blue eyes looking at me before his lashes lower and my own eyes flutter closed, shutting the world away.

And then we kiss. It is a universe long, an eternity of his

mouth moving softly against mine, slow exploration that makes my insides burn, and I want to get lost in it, in him, and never come back.

His seatbelt creaks as he leans in closer, one hand touching my hair, and I hear myself breathing. I hear him breathing. Two of us, just the two of us, except it isn't.

There is Brianna, my best friend.

"Ryan," I say, my voice coming out like a crumpled ball of foil, and he rests his forehead against mine. His fingers are still touching my hair. I can feel them shaking.

"Sarah," he says again, and there is such sweetness in his voice, in him, and I have tasted it and I want to do it again and again and again until I can't think of anything or anyone else.

"I'm sorry," I say, and he starts to shake his head, his hair so soft against my skin, his forehead still touching mine, and my heart screams that I'm not sorry, I'm not sorry at all and maybe he isn't either.

But then he says, "I didn't mean . . ." his voice quiet, and no, of course he didn't mean it. He didn't mean for this to happen. He didn't mean for us to kiss.

He has Brianna.

"It's okay," I say, sitting up and smiling the smile I use when any of Brianna's boyfriends come to me upset, the smile that says I will listen and understand because that's what I do. "I know things are a little weird with you and Brianna now, and the thing is, Brianna thinks you're mad at her," I say, reminding myself that I have a best friend, that this is her boyfriend, and that—well, what else is there? "I know you aren't mad, but she's just . . ." I swallow. "She really likes you a lot, and so she worries."

Ryan looks away from me then, stares out the windshield onto our dark front lawn. "I'm not . . . I'm not mad at her. I just . . . Sarah, I really didn't mean—"

"I know," I say as fast I can, because I don't want him to say anything else. I don't want to hear what comes after "really didn't mean," especially when it's been said twice. And maybe my voice comes out a little bit too high, maybe it's a little rushed, but I can't sit here in the quiet dark of Ryan's car like this.

I don't want to hear it was a mistake even though . . .

It wasn't. Not for me, and so I get out of the car then, say, "Thanks again," without looking back, not slamming the door but closing it and walking away.

I won't turn around and look. I won't watch him go.

I don't, but I'm shaking when I get inside. Shaking from what just happened. From wanting what I shouldn't. From how happy I was talking to him.

From how easy it was to be with him.

From that kiss.

From how tonight, at the party, he mentioned last week and a moment that I've wanted to forget about.

But haven't been able to.

eight

Here's what happened, here's the moment that's been stuck in my head, the one he talked about at the party.

Maybe it's nothing, but I still think about it.

I've been thinking about it.

Last Tuesday, I went to Brianna's to drop off a bunch of clothes she'd left at my house. Mom had washed them, and I hauled them out of my car, checking to make sure Brianna's mother wasn't home before I rang the doorbell.

"Hey," Brianna said when she opened the door, and grinned when I said, "Your laundry, Your Majesty."

"I love your mother," she said. "And you too. But you know that. Come on in."

"I don't want to bother you," I said, and Brianna shook her head, said, "Don't worry, Mom's at work. At least have a soda or something. I did the shopping, so there's more to drink than Ancient Secret diet tea."

"Deal," I said, and walked into the house.

Saw Ryan sitting in the living room, on the sofa.

"Oh," I said. "I didn't know—I didn't see Ryan's car—I should go."

"Why?" Brianna said. "We're just hanging out."

"Oh," I said again, and then realized there were other people in the living room too. Shelby and Henry and Terry were there, people Brianna was in plays with every year, and all of them were holding scripts and looking annoyed at me.

"Sorry," I said, and Brianna said, "No, it's good you're here. You can hang out with Ryan because he's totally bored, I can tell, and being too nice to say it. Plus he has to take everyone home because I promised he would after they all showed up. And as for not seeing his car—well, I made him park it down the street so I won't have to look at it."

And before I knew it, I was drinking root beer and sitting next to Ryan while everyone but me and him talked, and then it was just us; Brianna and Shelby and Henry and Terry all heading out onto the deck to do a scene, Shelby saying, "Outside! That's the kind of sets we should ask for!"

"Sorry," I said again, like it was all I could say. "I didn't know— I thought Brianna was by herself."

"I could tell," Ryan said. "I told her I wanted to talk when I came over tonight, and the next thing I know, I'm in the living room with you."

"Sorry," I said for what I figured was the thousandth time, and Ryan said, "No, I didn't mean—it's nice sitting with you. I mean—you know what I mean."

"Making the best of a bad situation?" I said, and made myself smile.

"No," he said, looking at me, and I wanted to look away from his eyes because they were so there and so blue and he was so gorgeous but I couldn't look away, I had to look at him because I spent so much time making sure I wasn't staring, that I was acting like he was just another guy. "I mean it's nice to be . . . I don't mind being with you at all. I like it."

"Yeah, me too," I said, still making myself smile and trying not to read anything into what he said. It was stupid to do that and I knew it. I also knew I should get up and go. But I didn't move, and he said, "Unless I'm getting ready to puke over a boat railing, right?" and I stopped thinking about leaving at all.

"You remember that?"

"It was only last year."

"I know," I said, and my voice came out so steadily, so calmly, but inside I was shaking.

"I didn't know boats could make people that sick," he said. "I swear the only thing that kept me from throwing myself overboard was talking to you. How come you never got those sneakers with dots on them?"

Oh wow, he remembered. Really remembered.

"I did," I said. "They didn't—well, they didn't look like I thought they would. They looked like a rash. On shoes. It wasn't pretty. I can't believe you listened to me babble about dots when you felt so bad."

"Are you kidding? You were the best thing about that trip."

"The best?" I said, and there was this . . . silence. It was weirdly tense in a way that made my toes curl.

"Second best, you mean," I said to stop that silence. To stop myself from looking at him and wishing. "Getting off the boat has to be first."

Outside, I heard Brianna say, "Shelby, you have to relax when you dance with Henry. Swing your hips a little. Yeah, like—okay, not that much."

"You should go practice with them," I said because I wanted that silence again, wanted it way, way too much. "Show Shelby how to dance properly."

"I can't dance."

"Well, not like Brianna. No one can. But you just have to hold her, not keep up with her."

"No, for real. I can't." He stood up and did . . . something. I think it might have been dancing, but it looked more like a fit of some kind.

The awful thing was, I still thought he looked cute.

"See? I suck," he said.

"No, you—okay, you really sort of do," I said, and we both laughed as he sat back down, our shoulders bumping as he settled onto the sofa.

"Told you," he said. "Remember how I asked you to that dance in eighth grade? I bet you're glad you were spared that night."

Still laughing and thinking of how stupid—and yet adorable—he looked, I said, "No, I would have loved it, I . . ." and trailed off, hearing what I was saying. "More like you were spared, because—well, I've seen my eighth-grade photo. You've seen it too. Not good at all."

He shook his head. "No, I wanted to go with you. I wished . . ."

And then there was silence again, *that* silence, and I realized how close we were. How easy it was to sit with him. To smile at him. To talk to him.

And then I heard Brianna laugh, heard her say, "I know, Ryan's great. Almost two months together now," and remembered exactly where I was.

Who I was.

And who I wasn't.

I stood up and said, "I better go, and hey, congrats on almost two months, I remember the night you guys got together and it's great, so great."

"Sarah," he said, standing up too, and I left the room, called out, "See you later!" and went out onto the deck, told Brianna I had to go and hugged her, then drove home and told myself all the things I'd thought were just that. Things that only I thought, and nothing more.

But now—

Now tonight has happened.

And while I know he's gone back to Brianna, I still—

I wish.

nine

I don't sleep much, alternating between joy (the kiss!) and terror (the kiss!), and half expect Brianna to come over and—well, I don't know what she'll do if she knows. Did Ryan tell her? I know he wouldn't make it sound like I kissed him—he's not that kind of guy—but how do you tell your girlfriend that you and her best friend kissed in a way that doesn't sound as terrible as it is?

I finally fall asleep after the sun rises, exhausted. The kiss almost seems like a dream now.

But it wasn't. It was real and it happened, and Brianna comes over just as I'm dragging myself downstairs to find Mom plating her chocolate pecan caramel rolls, which is cook-off speak for putting the food onto a plate.

"What's up with you?" Brianna says when I open the door. "You look awful."

"Tired," I say.

She gives me a look.

My insides quake. She knows, she knows, she knows.

"Well, can I come in or what?" she says, and as I nod, still waiting for her real reaction, she walks into the house, face lighting up.

"I smell food," she says, clapping her hands, and heads straight for the kitchen.

"Hey," she says when she gets there, waving at my mother, who says, "Look at you! I think you get prettier every day. You want a roll?"

Brianna shakes her head and sits down at the kitchen table.

"Where's the Professor?" she says, and I gesture toward the living room, where I can hear the sounds of Dad laughing over some old sitcom.

What is Brianna waiting for? Why is she acting so normal?

"What do you think?" Mom says, holding out the platter, and I say, "Gorgeous," and snatch a roll, breaking off a piece and eating it. I'm light-headed, shaky, and tense, so tense I can feel the muscles in the backs of my legs shaking.

"You don't think it needs a little more—something green on the side as a garnish, maybe, to make the rolls pop? Color is always good. Or maybe some orange zest on top?"

How am I supposed to do this? How can I be regular old Sarah, nice old boring Sarah, when Brianna must know and is keeping quiet for some reason?

I glance at her, but she's looking at the platter as if she is actually thinking about it.

I can't take this.

"It looks like something out of a cookbook," I say to Mom. "Really professional." She grins, and then heads off to show Dad.

Then Brianna finally turns to me, finally says, "Can we go upstairs?"

I nod, stomach sinking, and follow her up the stairs with my vision going all swirly with worry and the sugar rush.

In my room, I swallow, waiting.

Brianna flops on my bed and says, "So, what's wrong with Ryan?"

"I didn't mean—wait, what?" This isn't what she's supposed to say.

"What's wrong with Ryan?" she says again. "He didn't say anything last night about being mad at me. Or his hair, but that's not such a big deal. Did you actually talk to him at all?"

"Yes," I say, and the half-truth is bitter on my tongue. "Brianna, I—okay, I have to—"

"Well, at least you said something," she says, and sits up, shaking her hair back. As she does, I notice she's got a nice-sized hickey, the edge of it just visible where her shirt gaps a little at the neck.

"What's that?" I say, and she gives me a what-do-you-mean look, like I can't see the hickey, and of course Ryan didn't tell her about the kiss. He just went back to the party and saw her and realized how stupid he'd been and then kissed her once, twice, a million times, not one quick kiss but endless ones. Ones that marked her as his.

"Okay, you're freaky staring," she says, and touches her neck. Her fingers freeze on the mark.

"Oh, damn," she says, and gets up, rushes over to my dresser mirror. "I thought this shirt would cover it. Do you have any concealer?"

I shake my head and she frowns. "Does your mom?"

"Maybe, but what does it matter? Ryan won't care." It is so hard to get the words to come out light, normal.

She looks down at my dresser, blushing, and I stare at her.

"Brianna?"

"Don't say it, okay?" she mutters. "I know I was stupid, I know I shouldn't have let Greg—"

"Greg?" *Greg?*

She glances at me in the mirror and then comes back to the bed, flinging herself across it.

"Yeah," she says. "I just . . . we were dancing, and he was telling me how great I looked and I hugged him and then he was all, 'Hey, let's get some air,' and then we . . . well, we might have made out a little." Her voice gets all low and fast on the last words.

"You and Ryan broke up?" My mind is on overload because they broke up and that's terrible because Brianna really likes him, but can I call him? Would that be okay?

"We didn't break up," she says, and my heart stutter-stops in my chest, my breath catching.

"You didn't? But Greg and you—"

She shakes her head. "I made sure Ryan didn't see the hickey, okay? I told him to take me home and that I couldn't talk because I had a headache. And he can't know about me and

Greg, okay? I don't want to break up. I like him so much, Sarah, but he—lately, we haven't really been, you know. Doing much."

"You aren't . . . doing much?" I echo like a parrot, a trapped bird.

"Yeah, and I don't get it," she says. "At first I thought it was, I don't know, nice that he wasn't always trying to get me to do stuff right away. But he—we kiss but that's about it, and he's just . . . I don't know." She looks at her hands, which are clutching my bedspread. "I think I like him more than he likes me. What do I do?"

I stare at her. "What do you mean?"

"You always like guys more than they like you. What do you do about it? How do you stand it?"

Ouch. But the thing is, it's true.

It still stings, though. A lot.

"Well, every guy I've liked has always liked you more," I say, sitting down next to her, and it's true, so horribly true, but I can't cry now. I can't. "The ones that just want to hang out with me to be near you—well, I've gotten really good at figuring that out, and the rest . . ." I trail off, because there haven't been any "rest." There's been two guys. Two.

And Brianna only knows about one of them. Sam.

Last year, I liked Sam, who was new and from New York City and wrote great short stories and who didn't seem to notice Brianna whenever we were talking and she'd come by. I could tell it threw Brianna some, that he seemed totally immune to her, and I—well, I liked being the girl who was wanted.

And then Homecoming happened. Sam asked me to go to the

dance with him, and even though everyone says they hate the Homecoming dance because it's incredibly stupid, it's sort of stupid cool because you have to buy a nice dress and you get to see guys wearing things other than jeans and T-shirts. It's old-fashioned, but somehow it's okay. Nice, even.

I was really excited. I went dress shopping with Brianna, and not just to grab anything because the guy I was going with was someone she dumped and I was going out of pity, but to get something amazing. I didn't look as good as Brianna, of course—she got this short, tight, red dress that made even the salesgirl say, "Wow," when she came out of the dressing room—but I looked pretty.

Or at least I thought I did. Sam even said I did when he picked me up, and again when we danced in the crappily decorated gym to music that was muted by all the sound-proofing the school had put in.

And then I went to the bathroom.

On my way back, I saw two people talking in a corner outside the gym entrance. One of them was Brianna—I could see flashes of her red dress—and I grinned and headed toward her, wanting to tell her about dancing with Sam.

And then I saw she was with Sam, and he was smiling at her like he'd never smiled at me.

"You know you're the hottest thing here tonight," he said, and ran a hand down her arm. "Say you'll dance with me. I know you don't give a shit about the guy you're with."

I stood there, stunned, and watched Brianna smile. "Hot? Me? Since when? And what about Sarah?"

"She's not hot," he said, and I started to cry—just stood there and burst into tears, wondering if anything he'd said to me was ever real—and Sam looked up and said, "Oh shit," and walked off. Just left, and Brianna came over to me and said, "Sarah?" like she was terrified, like it was her fault Sam wanted her, not me, and I looked at her, so beautiful, and hated her.

Really and truly hated her. My best friend.

I ran then—in heels and everything—and Brianna came after me, got her date to give her his car and followed me in it, driving slowly as I walked out of the parking lot, still crying, furious with Sam and even with Brianna, as if it was her fault she was prettier than me, as if she'd made Sam say all the things he had.

"I shouldn't have agreed to talk to him," she said from the car as it rolled along slowly beside me. "I'm really sorry, Sarah. I thought he wanted to talk about you. He seemed to like you so much."

"I thought he did, but I guess he likes you more," I said, looking at her, still so furious, tears streaming down my face, and then she started to cry too, said, "I am so, so sorry, please don't be mad, please don't hate me," over and over until her voice broke.

I ended up driving us both back to my house in her date's car. Dad and Mom took the car back to the dance, and me and Brianna stayed up until almost four talking about what a jerk Sam was. It hurt for ages when I saw him at school, but after a while it hurt less, especially when I finally got to hear him read one of his short stories and it was really awful.

The only other guy I've liked is Ryan. Brianna knows about it, but doesn't. She thinks it was an eighth-grade thing, a forgotten thing. I don't know if she even remembers it at all.

But I do. And I still like him. And we kissed and—

"Hello, Sarah, are you listening?" Brianna says, waving a hand in front of my face. "I didn't mean what I said like how it sounded. I just don't know what to do about Ryan, how to keep him with me. And then the Greg thing . . ." She sighs again and rolls onto her back.

I would never kiss someone else if I got to kiss Ryan.

I shake my head, trying to erase that thought, and Mom knocks on my door. "Just wanted to see if you two need anything."

"We're fine," I say, voice tight, and Mom says, "All right, I'm just checking."

"I love your parents," Brianna says, her voice low. "I wish they were mine."

I shrug and try not to stare at her hickey. I try not to think about how she has Ryan and still turned to someone else.

I try not to think about how his mouth felt on mine.

"Hey, my mom's taking me to meet my dad today," she says, her voice still low. "Do you—do you want to come?"

I look at her. She is staring out my window now, twisting and untwisting her hair around one hand. Her fingers are shaking a little.

"Sure," I say, and she hugs me and tells me it will be fun.

We both know this is a lie.

ten

My parents are fine with me going to Brianna's, although my father reminds me to come home for dinner.

"Well, you don't have to," Mom says, but I know how much this cook-off means to her and say, "I will."

She sighs and says, "Good. I want to test my pizza recipe one more time. You don't mind, do you?"

I shake my head, because although beans and pizza do not sound like a good fit, it's pretty hard to object to pizza with what is essentially seven-layer dip on top.

Brianna's house is being cleaned when we get there, and she stops and talks to the two women doing it, who are in the kitchen scrubbing the countertops.

"I thought you were taking today off to go to Luke's soccer

game," she says to one of them, who shakes her head and says, "Our car broke down again, so . . ." and shrugs. The other one, who is older and has hair that has been bleached white, with thick black eyebrows that are all the more obvious because she has bangs that swoop down to meet them, says, "Thanks for the other day."

Brianna shakes her head. "It was nothing. Is my mom . . . have you seen her?"

Black eyebrows shakes her head. "Heard her, though. Been upstairs since we came."

Brianna nods and says, "Let's get ready," to me.

"So, what did you do?" I ask her as we're heading up to her room, and she looks back over her shoulder at me.

"About what?"

"The woman in the kitchen thanked you—"

Brianna waves a hand at me, dismissal. "What, Gloria? I just drove her and her mother to the doctor the other afternoon."

"It was nice of you," I say, and Brianna shrugs.

"It wasn't a big deal. I didn't want to do my homework and I really wanted a cheeseburger, so it wasn't like I wasn't going out anyway."

This is classic Brianna. She will do something nice and then swear she did it because she had something else to do, and the nice thing just happened. We became friends because of it, actually.

In kindergarten, my best friend was Meredith, who told me we were best friends on the first day of school and who knocked out someone's front tooth with a tetherball "by accident" on the second. I was terrified of her, which Meredith

53

liked because it meant she could tell me what to do all the time—which she did.

By the time I'd been in kindergarten for a month, I'd been to the doctor twice, once because I shoved a piece of foam up my nose (Meredith had told me to) and another because I'd gotten something stuck in my ear (again, foam and Meredith) and was waking up every morning with a stomachache.

I'd come into class one day, trembling a little as I waited for Meredith to come find me, and Brianna came up to me and said, "I lost my pencil. It has a star on it. Will you help me look for it?"

"No," Meredith said, coming up to us, and Brianna didn't even look at her, just smiled at me and said, "Please?"

I nodded, because of course I wanted to help Brianna look for her pencil. She was pretty. Everyone wanted to play with her. And she never, ever made anyone shove foam up their nose. Or in their ear.

"No," Meredith said again, very loudly this time, and gave me a you're-going-to-get-pinched look.

"She has to," Brianna said, and finally looked at Meredith. "Mrs. Johnson said so when I asked her."

"No, she didn't," Meredith said.

"Go ask her," Brianna said, and Meredith frowned, looked toward our teacher—who wasn't all that fond of Meredith—and then said, "A pencil with a star on it is stupid, just like you."

"Come on," Brianna said to me, like Meredith hadn't said a word, and when I followed her to look for the pencil, she whispered that she actually had an extra one, and did I want it?

I nodded, and when she gave it to me she said, "Will you sit next to me during story time?" and just like that, I didn't have to do everything with Meredith anymore.

I was free, and Brianna was the one who did it. She saved me.

Once, when we were in fifth grade, I asked her why she'd come up to me that day. She looked at me like I was crazy and then said, "Because Meredith was so mean to you! And besides, I had a pencil I wanted to get rid of, remember?"

I'd nodded and looked at Brianna's dresser, where I knew she kept her important stuff, and saw the pencil with the star on it by a small stuffed cat her father had given her. I loved her so much then, and I still have my star pencil at home, tucked into a desk drawer.

"Well?" Brianna says now, and I look at her. At the girl who was kind to me because she saw I needed someone to help me. At the person who knows me so well and who's been such a huge part of my life that hanging out with other people has never seemed important or even necessary.

I smile at her and she points at her neck. "Do you see it?"

"No," I say because she's covered the hickey up, made it disappear. "It's gone."

And it is, not just because of the makeup, but because I won't think about it again.

I also won't think about kissing Ryan again.

I'll be a true best friend again.

"Good," she says, and then stills as we hear footsteps in the hall. I watch her turn toward the door, waiting, and see her swallow as the steps pass, heading downstairs.

"We'd better go," she says after a moment, and I nod.

Her mother isn't downstairs, and the cleaning people, who are now gathering up their stuff and getting ready to go, tell Brianna she's outside.

"You look nice," the woman with the kid who plays soccer says, and the other one, the one with the eyebrows, says, "She's right, you do."

"Thanks," Brianna says. "Did you get . . . everything?"

The women nod, and the one with the black eyebrows waves a white envelope at her.

"Great," Brianna says. "I'm sorry about last time. If I'd had enough money—" She glances at me. "I'm just sorry Mom was so busy at work that she couldn't take my calls."

"Don't worry about it, honey," the woman with the black eyebrows says. "You're not supposed to pay us. See you next week?"

Brianna nods and then heads toward the deck that's at the back of her house, opening the glass door that leads out onto it. I follow reluctantly, and squint as I walk out into the sunshine.

Brianna's mother is standing on the deck, very carefully inspecting her outfit, smoothing the sleeves of the black silk blouse she has on.

"I don't think the dry cleaner pressed this properly. These cuffs don't look pressed at all to me. Do they look pressed to you, Brianna?"

"They look great. You look great," Brianna says, and her mother shrugs and looks at her feet.

"What about my shoes? I got them yesterday and they looked wonderful in the store—the saleswoman said they were made for my feet—but now I'm thinking maybe they're a bit too pointy. I don't want my feet to look pointy."

"They don't, Mom," Brianna says. "You really do look great. Where are we meeting Dad?"

"Hmmmm?" her mother says, and finally looks at Brianna. "Oh, Brianna, I've told you not to wear that color eye shadow. It makes you look tired."

"Sorry," Brianna says. "Where are we meeting Dad?"

"If he comes, we're meeting him at that coffee shop over on Patterson."

"If he comes?"

"Well, I had to call the lawyer again," Brianna's mother says. "Your father's late with his child support payment again, never mind that I have you to raise plus work and don't have time to remind him of his responsibilities."

"Oh," Brianna says. "I—I'll call him to see if he's coming."

"I might as well go to work, then, because things there are crazy, like always, and I've got a ton of stuff to get done before next week's meeting. Call me if he's going to show and I'll—well, we'll get you there because he and I need to talk and he'll avoid me, like always, unless I'm with you." She kisses Brianna's cheek before breezing past me into the house.

Brianna looks out at her yard, her back very stiff, and I know she is trying not to cry. I know she needs a minute, because she always needs a minute after she talks to her mother. Just being near her mother makes me feel miserable. I don't know how Brianna stands it.

I look back inside her house, see her mother back her car out of the garage and leave.

"I'd better call my dad," Brianna says a moment later, her voice dull, her eyes not meeting mine, and I say, "Okay," and we head inside, walk to the kitchen.

Brianna calls her father while I sit at the kitchen table. The conversation is very brief.

"Hi, this is Brianna. Is my father there? Oh. Did he leave a number? He didn't? Okay, thanks. What? No, I'm fine. Thanks, Kerri. And tell my dad he shouldn't make you work weekends! Bye."

She hangs up and walks her fingers along the kitchen counter.

"He's busy," she says after a minute. "He's showing a bunch of houses today. Kerri says it was a last minute thing." She looks at me. "I bet you anything they'll end up going to court again."

"Oh, Brianna," I say, getting up and giving her a hug. "I'm sorry."

"Me too," she says. "It's getting so the only time I see Dad is when Mom makes me come to court with her so she can show the judge she's raising a teenager on her own and isn't getting paid nearly enough to do it."

"We could go find him," I say, and she shakes her head.

"If he wanted to see me, he'd see me," she says. "Can we go back to your house?"

"Sure," I say, and I do know how Brianna stands life with her mother. How she stands never seeing her father.

She has no choice.

eleven

Back at my house, Brianna helps my mother go through her serving platters again and I watch them, my mother asking Brianna about school and Ryan, Brianna glowing from the attention.

"Well, it'll be eight weeks pretty soon," she says. "That's the longest I've ever gone out with anyone. We're going to have a two-month anniversary!"

"He seems very nice," Mom says, carefully looking over another platter.

"He is," Brianna says. "The day after we talked for the first time, he actually tracked me down here and called. Isn't that sweet?"

I swallow and look at my hands. They are clenched into fists on the table. I force myself to relax them.

"It is sweet," Mom says. "Sarah Bear, what are you doing tonight?"

"Homework."

"You can't do homework by yourself on a Saturday night," Brianna says. "You can hang out with me and Ryan."

No. No no no no no no.

"Right, because every date needs three people," I say.

"We're just going to do homework at my house," Brianna says, and looks at Mom. "I swear, Ryan studies even more than Sarah. Sometimes when I'm around them I can feel myself getting smarter. So really, I need her around all the time, don't I?"

"Well, I think you're very smart already," Mom says, and Brianna smiles, blindingly bright, so happy.

"Really?"

"Of course. But if you want Sarah to come over, it's fine with me, and thank you for helping me go through all my platters."

"I like doing stuff like this," Brianna says, and grins at me. "See? Your mother wants you to come." She gets up and tugs me to my feet. "Let's go up to your room. I need to fix my eye shadow and stuff."

"Okay, why do you want me around again when you're supposed to be with Ryan?" I say when we're in my room and she's borrowed some of my mother's eye shadow.

"I just thought it would be fun for us to hang out like we did last night."

"But we didn't really hang out last night," I say. "We went to a party." I try not to look at her neck. Try not to think about anything at all.

"We did too hang out. We watched a movie before, remember? And it's not like you haven't come out with us before. You even went bowling with us on our first date, remember? Well, not our official first date, but you know. You were there."

"Everyone was there, Brianna. It was the school fundraiser. My parents were even there!"

That night . . . I do remember it. I remember how Brianna had come with us because her mother was working late, like always, and so me and her and my parents had been bowling. My parents were even both bowling pretty well—for them—and then Ryan had come over and said hello.

"Hey, Sarah, Brianna," he'd said. "How's it going?"

"Okay," I'd mumbled, thinking of the party we'd all been at last night. Of how he'd talked to me and then gone off with Brianna.

Of how he'd called my house that morning and I'd thought, for one crazy second, that he'd called to talk to me, but when Brianna heard me say, "Ryan?" she'd grabbed my arm, grinning, and whispered, "Sarah, he's called me *here*! And after I just barely mentioned that I'd probably see you today. He totally likes me." And so I'd said, "Hold on, Brianna's here," and handed the phone to her, pasting a smile on my face as Brianna had laughed and talked and ended by saying, "Well, maybe I'll see you tonight at the bowling thing," and twirled around in a circle after she'd hung up the phone.

"Everything's suddenly looking a lot better," Brianna had said to Ryan then, as Dad bowled yet another gutter ball, and I'd watched Ryan flush and say, "Oh. Um. Thanks," before I'd gotten up and pretended I wanted to watch my mother try not to land her bowling ball right in the gutter too.

I'd ended up spending most of the night practically glued to my parents, pretending I didn't see Brianna and Ryan talking just a few feet away from me.

Ryan had tried to act like he wasn't just there for Brianna, which was nice of him, but his silly questions (How are you? Are you having fun? Did you have fun last night? I was sorry we couldn't talk more—which wasn't a question and was just him being nice since he'd ended up leaving with Brianna as soon as she'd come in and seen him) were all he asked, like Brianna had him so tongue-tied he couldn't think of anything to say other than the same stuff over and over.

Finally, Brianna had said, "Uh oh. See how Sarah's face is all squinty, Ryan? She only looks like that when she's upset. Sarah, is he wrecking your bowling concentration?"

"Oh," Ryan had said to me. "I didn't mean to—I mean, obviously I was talking, but I didn't mean to bother you."

"I'm fine," I'd said as carefully as I could, and watched Brianna whisper something in Ryan's ear.

Ryan had flushed, but then looked at Brianna. She'd smiled her smile—*the* smile—at him, and when they left a few minutes later I'd pretended I was fine. I'd hugged her automatically but didn't listen to what she whispered in my ear. I couldn't bear to hear it.

I'd pretended she didn't take Ryan's arm and walk away with him.

I'd cried for what felt like forever that night, but it wasn't forever. I'd learned that when Brianna came over the next day and told me everything that had happened.

I'd sat there, listening to her talk about Ryan until I was sure I was a thousand years older and the universe was on the edge of dying, but only an hour had passed. Just one little hour, and when Brianna left to go get ready to meet Ryan, who was taking her out for pizza ("Just him and me!"), I'd curled up in a ball on my bed and waited to cry again.

I never did. I was too sad for tears, hurt in a deep, nameless way that made me feel ashamed (Brianna was my best friend) and angry (I'd talked to him first! Why couldn't he have wanted to keep talking to me? Why?)—and in the end, I just pushed it all away.

"Hey, you gotta get ready to go," Brianna says now. "Oh! You should wear your purple shirt. It looks nice on you."

"I really don't think I should come over," I say, sitting down on my bed. "Last night was weird enough and—"

"Weird? Why was it weird? Did Ryan and I seem weird? Did he seem weird?"

"No," I say automatically, to stop the worry in her voice.

"Something was weird, I know it," she says. "Your face is all squinchy and I know what that means. Are you sure he didn't say anything about me to you?"

"Does it really matter?" I say, my voice rising. "I mean, hello, it's not like you were thinking about him all night, Brianna. You were off with Greg, remember?"

"I wasn't with him," she says, her voice sharp. "It was just . . . you know how stuff happens sometimes, right?" She walks away from the dressers, sits next to me. "Okay, maybe you don't know, but if you were dancing with a really cute guy and he was telling you how great you are—you wouldn't like that?"

Part of me wants to scream, "No, I wouldn't! Because I'd be happy with Ryan!" but another part of me knows exactly what she's talking about. Remembers how I wished for things I shouldn't have last night.

How I did things I shouldn't have last night.

"I might like it," I mutter, and she sighs and rests her head on my shoulder.

"It's not Ryan who's being weird," she says. "Well, it is, but it's . . . okay. Yesterday, he told me he wanted to talk at school, and I know what that means. He's done it before and I just—I'm the one who says I want to talk. I'm the one who . . ." She sits up and sniffs once, looking at my bedspread. "He can't break up with me, Sarah. I like him and I don't . . . I don't want it to be over yet. That's why you have to come tonight. If you're there, the two of us can't talk, and I'm going to make him remember why we first got together. I'm going to make him see how great we are, and then everything will be fine."

"But—" Could she really be right? Could Ryan want to break up with her? Brianna's never lost any guy until she's wanted them gone.

"So will you come over tonight? Please? Pretty please?" she says, and Brianna, always-perfect, always-knows-what-to-do Brianna, has tears in her eyes.

I nod and she hugs me. "Thank you. All you have to do is hang out with us, and that's not a big deal, right? Besides, it's not like you have anything to do anyway."

"Right," I say, and swallow around the lump that's risen in my throat at the reminder that I have no social life.

"Hey, don't say it like that. You just need a guy to like you and it'll happen. You'll see." She blinks really fast at me. "How does the eye shadow look?"

"Gorgeous," I say, and stand up, look at myself in the mirror. "How about me? How do I look?"

"Like Sarah," she says, and comes and stands behind me, hugging me and grinning at our reflection. "Like my best friend."

Not gorgeous. Not even pretty. I look like myself, whatever that means.

I know what it means, and it's nothing good. It's ordinary. Boring.

Alone.

twelve

Brianna's house is quiet and empty, and I stand hesitantly in the kitchen while she checks her messages.

Brianna's house is normal enough looking—Brianna drops things on the floor, her mother leaves half-eaten tins of the mints she always has with her everywhere—but I've still never felt comfortable here.

I don't think Brianna does either.

But now I feel even more uncomfortable than usual. I can't believe Ryan is coming over. I can't believe I'm here. Why did I ever agree to this again?

Because I want to see him.

I'm not here for Brianna. I'm here for me, and I'm terrible. I'm terrible and no kind of friend at all and I—

I can't help it. I still want to see him.

Brianna hangs up the phone and starts playing with the burners on the stove, flipping them on until red circles glow, lighting the stove, and then flipping them off.

"Do you know some stoves have things on them?" she says. "Like, sticky-up things that you put pans on."

Of course I do—my mother has a gas stove—but Brianna's mouth is pinched tight and she is blinking very fast, the way she does when she wants to be mad but is actually sad.

"What happened when you checked your messages?" I say.

Brianna frowns.

"Oh, the usual. Mom's working late and, by the way, she thinks I look like I've put on a little weight, and Dad didn't call." She sighs and gently kicks the bottom of the oven with one foot. "Why do my parents hate me?"

"They don't hate you," I say. "Your mom is—she's just how she is, and doesn't your dad always stay away if it looks like there's going to be another court thing?"

"There's always another court thing," Brianna says. "I'm like this bone he and Mom fight over. Sometimes I think I could be a dog or a vase and they'd still act exactly the same." She looks at me. "And don't lie and say it's not true."

"They know you're not a dog or a vase," I say, and I'm not lying. I do think Brianna's parents know she exists and that she's their daughter.

I just don't think either of them cares. She's not important to them like she should be, and I know it's really hard on her.

I go over to where she's standing and put an arm around her. "You're better than both of them."

"You think?"

"Totally."

"I'd never treat my kid like they—when I have kids, I'm going to make them love me more than anything."

"You won't have to make them love you, Brianna. They just will."

"No, sometimes you have to make people love you."

"You can't *make* someone love you."

"Of course you can. You just be who they want you to be and eventually they will."

"That's . . ." Awful, I want to say, but the look on Brianna's face, a mixture of anger and helplessness, stops me. "But what about being yourself?"

"What good is that?" she says. "I mean, look at you. You're tiny and quiet, so guys never notice you. It's because they're stupid and only think about looks and stuff, of course, but still."

"Right," I say, stung, and my voice cracks.

"Don't be sad," Brianna says. "It'll be different eventually, I'm sure of it. Plus your parents love you in an insanely awesome way, and you know I love you. If I could have a sister, it would totally be you, but I like to think we're already sisters. Don't you think that?"

"Yeah," I say, but I wonder if there are sisters out there where one feels like she's a shadow of the other. If there's a girl with a sister who sometimes makes her feel like nothing.

"Oh crap, Ryan's gonna be here soon," Brianna says. "Wait down here and let him in for me? I have to go get ready."

"But you look great," I say, panicked. I want to see him, but I don't want to be alone with him!

"I have to look perfect," she says. "All you have to do is talk to him for a few minutes."

"Brianna—"

"Fine, don't talk. Just do homework with him. You can do that, right? You were going to do homework tonight anyway."

"Brianna," I say again, but she races upstairs, calling out, "You're the most awesomest ever, Sarah Bear," and I know that nothing short of Ryan himself going upstairs will get her to come down before she's ready.

I grab my homework and try to figure out where to sit. On the weird little bench by the front door?

No, because then it will look like I'm waiting for him and I—

Well, the thing is, I am.

thirteen

I end up sitting at the kitchen table, and when the doorbell rings I jump up right away and then want to kick myself when I open the door and Ryan says, "This is new. I always have to ring the doorbell more than once before you . . . oh. Sarah. Hi."

"Hey," I say, and look at the floor, not him. "Brianna's upstairs getting ready. She'll be down in a minute and then you two . . . anyway. She'll be down soon."

"Oh. Okay," he says, and shoves his hair off his forehead with one hand. It flips back down right away, and I watch the inky strands fall with a greed that frightens me. I don't usually look at him for so long, but I've been waiting and wishing he was here to see me and now he's blushing a little and I want to touch him so bad my stomach is all hot and fluttery with it, my fingers trembling.

"We should sit down," I say at the same time he says, "You wanna sit down?" and we don't sit, we both smile and we are standing here, smiling at each other.

It's Ryan, I tell myself, just Ryan. I can do this. I've known him forever and we're friends and he's dating my best friend. And I have to do this, be normal. Stop staring. Stop wishing.

I point at the sitting room no one in Brianna's house ever sits in, and he shakes his head and whispers, "I'm actually sort of scared of that room."

"Me too," I say, and we're still grinning at each other. It's like I can't stop smiling, and he looks happy, like he's glad to be here. I could reach out and touch his hand. He's that close. I could touch his hand and slide my fingers up his arm and he would lean in toward me and—

"I'll be right down!" Brianna calls from upstairs, and of course he's smiling and glad to be here. His girlfriend is here.

I turn around and head for the living room, blinking back a stupid rush of tears that make my eyes burn, and after a moment I hear him follow.

I sit in the recliner, so he and Brianna can have the sofa, and then say, "Oh, my books, I have to get them," and head for the kitchen so I won't have to look at him anymore. I'll go back out there and be pure of heart and mind, I swear. I just need a second. Or twelve.

In the kitchen, I pick up my stuff and then walk over to the fridge and rest my head against it. Then I grab three sodas—two grape and one root beer—and head back to the living room.

I'm calm. I'm relaxed. This will be fine.

Except it isn't.

Silence falls as I pass him his soda, a silence I am familiar with, a silence I *know*, and I look at him, see him glance away like he was looking at me, throat working as he swallows.

Brianna comes down, finally, and as she does I'm sure she must see how hard I'm trying not to look at Ryan and how he's so careful not to look at me.

I take a sip of my soda. My throat feels thick, clogged, and it is so hard to swallow that tiny bit of liquid.

"So, hi," Brianna says to both of us. "That's what you say when someone comes in, you know? Why are you both so quiet?"

"I . . . is that the only root beer?" Ryan says, and I shake my head because I don't trust myself to say anything.

"Well, I guess that counts as talking," Brianna says, and grins at Ryan. "Lucky you, you get a kiss." She leans in toward him.

Ryan stands up, and Brianna freezes.

"I'm going to get another soda," he says, and heads for the kitchen.

"I'll come with you," Brianna says.

"It's okay, I'll be right back," he says, and Brianna smiles and says, "Hurry," her voice playful, but when he's gone she looks at me and whispers, "You saw that, right?"

"I . . . sorry," I say, and I am, but not like she thinks.

I'm sorry Ryan and I kissed but not as sorry as I should be.

"Don't be. I'm fixing this," she says, and heads into the kitchen. After a second I hear noises; her voice, soft, and his voice, quiet too, and then total silence. Kissing silence. I put my soda down.

I've pushed the sides in, pressure from my hands.

Ryan comes back after a minute, his gaze darting to mine, and I see he's holding a root beer.

"I like it better than grape," he says, and there is something in his eyes, something—

Something that makes my breath catch, and suddenly last night is in the room with us, is all around us.

I make myself say, "Me too, obviously," and hold up my own can, covering the dents the best I can.

"I know," he says, and blushes.

Where is Brianna? What is she doing in the kitchen?

"Did you get started on the history reading?" he says, like he's trying to sound normal, but he doesn't, not at all, and I wonder what he's thinking.

"No, not yet," I say, and I don't sound normal either, call out, "Brianna?" because even though I'm fine sitting here with him, it's just . . . we're alone.

"I—last night," he says. "I . . . the thing is, I didn't mean for it to happen, but I—"

"What are you two looking so intense about?" Brianna says, and I look up and see she's standing in the doorway watching us. "And Sarah, I was gone for, like, two minutes, tops. Where did you think I was?"

"I . . . we were just waiting for you," I say quickly, words bubbling out of me. "You should sit down. On the sofa."

"You mean by my own boyfriend?" Brianna says, and looks at

Ryan, rolling her eyes, but then grins at me—and sits next to him.

"So, you ready to pay attention to me now?" she says, and kisses him. I stare at my history book and then open it. I'm not on the right page, but it doesn't matter. I'm not looking at it. I'm trying not to think about Brianna and Ryan kissing.

I'm trying not to wonder what he was going to say before she came in.

I'm trying not to think about how I know what his mouth feels like.

Tastes like.

I look up and Brianna is pouting a little, prettily, but her eyes are troubled and Ryan isn't kissing her, is opening his own history book. He looks at me, right at me, and then he swallows and looks away.

"We'd better get started," he says, and Brianna says, "I should have known having Sarah here would make you shy and all Mr. Study Guy. Sarah, you totally owe me one for taking my real boyfriend away."

"Yeah," I say around the lump in my throat. "I know I do."

fourteen

I start to relax a little once we've been working for a while. For all that Brianna doesn't care about homework, when it's something she wants to do, like the individual research reports we've all been assigned as part of this term, she goes the extra mile. Plus more.

In eighth grade, she did this amazing interactive project about Broadway. She wrote to actors and actresses who'd been greats in their day, and used their stories in an almost-book-length report about what Broadway represented to those who'd been part of the plays that made it great.

It was so good our English teacher wanted to talk to Brianna's mom about trying to get it published, but Brianna's mother was always busy, and at the end-of-the-year awards ceremony, she had to leave early, before Brianna even got her prize.

"There," she says, pushing away the book she's holding. "I know exactly what my project proposal is going to be now—the struggles of Broadway to keep up with the ever-growing ways people view media."

"Wow," I say, and she grins.

"I know! Good, right?"

"Very."

She stretches and leans into Ryan. "What are you doing?"

"I don't know yet. Maybe something about how artists function in a society where funding is harder and harder to find, and how there aren't any real stars in the field anymore. At least, not ones that everyone's heard of."

"Because there's no money in it, just like you said," Brianna says. "It's easy to be famous for just being someone, and that usually pays. Or at least gets you stuff." She looks at me. "What are you doing?"

I shrug, and Brianna nudges my leg with her foot, grinning.

"I know. It's shoes, of course. Your obsession. It's cute. Weird, but cute."

"I don't think it's weird," Ryan says. "I mean, I've never been to a Broadway show and you've been to, what, fifty? But I don't say you're obsessed."

"That's different," Brianna says, flushing. "Why are you being mean? Sarah, isn't he being mean?"

I know what I'm supposed to say. "Yes." I'm supposed to say, "Yes," and Brianna will say, "Thank you," all fake sadly, and then tease Ryan and press up against him and why—

Why does Brianna have to make me feel so bad sometimes?

"Fine, now you're both being mean," Brianna says, wrapping her arms around herself, which manages to make her look sad and presses her breasts up at the same time. "I'm sorry Broadway isn't as cool as your so-called art, Ryan. I'm sorry I don't want to read about shoes or spend ages making ones that no one will ever see because who looks at feet?"

"I need some air," Ryan says, and stands up abruptly, walking out of the room. After a second, I hear the deck door slam.

"Oh shit," Brianna says.

I look at the floor. "You think me liking shoes is weird? For real?"

"No," she says, looking away from the direction of the deck and shaking her head. "I mean, not really. It's different, but it works for you. Do you—what do you think I should do about Ryan? I mean, guys have gotten mad at me before, but it's always been for stuff like not wanting to be with them or talking to another guy. I don't get why he's upset. I didn't say anything bad about him or his art." She sucks on her bottom lip for a second. "Well, not really bad. Will you go talk to him? See how mad he is?"

"I don't see how I can . . . I really don't want to get involved, Brianna."

"Involved? Sarah, come on. You're just finding out if he's mad at me. It's asking a question, and you've done that before. Plus he didn't just walk out on you."

"He didn't walk out on you. He just went out on the deck, and maybe you should go out there and . . . "

I trail off as Brianna hugs her arms tighter around herself, not to show off her chest like before, but because she's really upset.

"I didn't tell you everything about last night," she says. "I asked . . . I asked Greg to go outside with me. I wanted to prove I could kiss someone else and it would be just like kissing Ryan. But it wasn't. I kept thinking about what he'd do if he saw me, and it wasn't like it would be with any other guy. I couldn't even . . . I couldn't even picture him getting mad or anything. I could just see him leaving and that—" She breaks off, looks at me. "I couldn't stand that. And I'm sorry about what I said before, about you and your shoes. You aren't mad at me, are you?"

"Just . . . hurt," I say, and Brianna looks at me, surprise all over her face.

"Oh," she says after a moment, her voice quiet. "I didn't . . . when I say stuff, I don't mean it if it sounds bad. You know that, right? I mean, I love you. You know that too, don't you?"

I nod, because I do, and Brianna smiles and gets up, nudging me with her knee when I don't follow.

"Go on," she says, happy again. "Talk to Ryan. I'm going to make something to eat for him. And for us too, of course."

I stare at her, jealous—and mad at myself for it—and she bites her lip. "I really am sorry. I'm a terrible person. You shouldn't hang out with me, and now you know why my parents never want to be around me."

Her voice cracks on the last words, and I know exactly why Brianna is the way she is, why she is so quick to throw out words that wound more than she knows. I know why she is so scared of being left.

She has been.

"Your parents suck. A lot," I say. "And I've wanted to hang out with you since we were in kindergarten."

"Really?"

I nod.

"Thanks," she whispers, hugging me, and then she lets go and spins me toward the deck, marching us both to the door that leads out onto it.

"Look at him," she says. "Isn't he cute?"

I look. He's standing out by the steps that lead into Brianna's backyard, head down, eyes closed. He looks tired and sad and I want to hug him and tell him everything will be all right.

"He's okay," I say, and Brianna laughs and opens the door, scooting me halfway through with a gentle nudge. Scooting me toward Ryan.

He turns as I do, and I take a step toward him. I hear Brianna humming, happy, as she closes the door, and I want to turn around and bang on it, beg her to let me back in.

But I want to stay out here more.

fifteen

"Ryan?" I say, and I hope it doesn't sound like my body is tingling just from saying his name.

"Hey," he says, half-turning toward me, and the light that is supposed to shine out onto the backyard and highlight potential burglars or the grass or whatever is only there for him right now, is only shining on him, and he is gorgeous and I kissed him.

I kissed him, and he kissed me, and I should have touched his hair, should have memorized the feel of his mouth. I should have done more than think *yes this is it, yes this is what I've been waiting for, this is how it's supposed to be*.

"Brianna's really worried," I say, the words coming out fast, like if I can get them out quick enough I will stop thinking. Stop wanting. "She likes you so much," and now my voice is cracking but I'm not sad, I'm not. I make myself smile, stretch my mouth wide. "She's even going to make you something to eat. She's never done that for another guy."

He looks at me, and I wonder if he can see inside my head, if he can see the words I haven't said out loud, that I don't dare say. *What was last night? Why did it happen?*

"Are you okay?" he says, still looking at me, and I feel my smile slip, fade, and the silence that falls over us then is so total I can't hear anything, not the rush-hiss of my heart pounding in my chest, not the sounds all around us; insects, wind, and the distant clatter of others' lives in houses built close but not too close because when we look out our windows we all like to pretend that everything we see is ours.

But Ryan is not mine.

"I'm fine," I say, and glance over my shoulder, catch a glimpse of Brianna moving around the kitchen, fluid grace even when doing something ordinary like making popcorn. She will put extra butter on because she knows I love it, and I know that about her just like I know she had chicken pox when she was four and has a scar on her left ankle from it, the one spot she scratched, her mother telling her she'd be ugly for doing it and making her cry.

"I'm fine," I say again, and this time when I look at Ryan I make myself see him with Brianna that first time, that first night at that party at the end of the summer, and then all the times past that; at school, after school, weeks of them together. Weeks.

I do it because I have to see what is real, and it's them.

"You should go inside and talk to her," I say. "I'll give you five minutes of privacy and then I'll come in and grab my stuff and take off."

He looks down at the deck. "Are you—?" He clears his throat. "Can I ask you something?"

Yes. No. Yes. I swallow, force myself to shrug, to say "okay" without words because right now I can't manage any.

"I—Sarah," he says, and takes a step closer. My toes curl inside my sneakers, waiting. Wanting whatever is coming. "I just . . . I have to know something. Do you—do you remember the party before school started? You were in the study and I came in and we were talking?"

I nod and he swallows. I see his throat work, pale skin caught by the glow of the light that shines out into the dark.

"I really wanted to keep talking to you," he says, the words coming out in a rush. "And when I called your house the next day, I didn't call for Brianna, Sarah. I wanted to talk to you."

"Me?" *Me?*

"Yes," he says, and his voice is rough, intense, and we are standing close enough to touch now but we aren't touching, we aren't, but I can feel how we could all around us. In every breath I take there is the promise of his skin touching mine and I want that. I want us to kiss again, I want him to kiss me, I want him.

I want him, and he is looking at me like he did last night.

He is looking at me like he wants to kiss me.

"Ryan," I say, and it comes out like a plea, and I am afraid of this, of him, of me, of him and me, but not enough, not like I should be, and his head lowers toward mine and I am rising up on my toes, rising to meet him, and then—

And then Brianna's mom yells, "Who the hell parked their car in my garage?"

sixteen

Brianna's mother is in the kitchen still yelling at Brianna, who is staring at a bowl of popcorn that's fallen to the floor. Ryan and I have just come into the house, the moment between us broken, both of us blinking and turning toward the door at the same time.

Both of us tensing at the sound of Brianna's mother's voice.

"Why did you park in the garage?" Brianna's mother says to her. "You know you aren't supposed to."

"You said you were working late and I—"

"Oh, so when I'm off trying to support us, you can't be bothered to walk up the front steps?"

"I'm sorry, Mom," Brianna says, bending down to pick up the scattered popcorn and the shattered bowl that once held it.

"And you're eating now? Brianna, sweetie, you shouldn't eat a thing after four. It'll go straight to your hips. Trust me, I know."

"Mom," Brianna says, not angrily, just sadly. "I've got—Ryan's here. And Sarah. Can we talk about this later?"

"Oh," Brianna's mother says. "Of course I'm bothering you. Well, don't worry about me. I don't need to eat or sit down and rest or anything."

I have to get to Brianna before this gets worse, I have to stop this, so I step into the kitchen and say, "Hey, Brianna, I was just talking to Ryan and—oh, you made popcorn. Thank you!"

I look at Brianna's mom and force myself to smile at her when I really just want to kick her for being so awful. "I get so hungry sometimes, and Brianna said she didn't want to mess with anything in the kitchen because you might want something when you got home, but I begged until she did."

"Well, there's no food now," her mother says. "Brianna's made a mess."

"It's not that bad," Ryan says, coming into the kitchen as well and looking at the floor. "You should see some of the stuff I've dropped in the kitchen."

"Oh, hello," Brianna's mother says, smiling at Ryan, lashes fluttering, and I watch Brianna grimace. "I just meant that it's such a mess to clean up spilled food. I sure wish there'd been boys who looked like you back when I was in school. It wasn't that long ago, you know."

Brianna rolls her eyes at that, and Ryan smiles tightly at her mom.

I kneel and start to pick up some of the popcorn and pieces of the bowl. Brianna drops down next to me, her hands shaking as she does the same.

"I'm exhausted," her mother says. "I'm going to bed. Brianna, don't be loud."

"I won't," Brianna says, and the three of us clean up silently.

"You'd better go," Brianna says when we're done, and Ryan says, "Are you sure you're okay?"

Brianna nods and kisses him. My stomach twists and I hate myself for it. Ryan glances at me and I look away, pretend I am still looking on the floor for missed bits of popcorn or bowl.

When he's gone, Brianna comes and stands next to me. She cries, biting her lip so she won't make any noise, and I hug her hard, wishing I could make Brianna's mother see what she does to her daughter.

Knowing that if I did, it wouldn't make a difference.

Brianna doesn't want to spend the night at my house, and I leave a few minutes later, telling her to call me if she needs anything. I hug my parents when I get home.

"I love you," I say.

"Well, of course you do, we're very lovable," Dad says, winking at me, and Mom smiles, says, "Henry!" and then, "Sarah, honey, is everything okay?"

I nod. It isn't, but looking at them makes me remember that when it comes to parents, I got lucky.

seventeen

Sunday mornings are always a big deal at my house. First, my mother wakes us up, and then we go to church. Mom likes to go to the early service because she—well, she just likes mornings, period.

Usually I'm too sleepy to do anything but try not to fall asleep, but now I can't stop thinking about last night. About Brianna's mom. About how Brianna looked when her mother was talking to her, tired and sad and defeated in a way Brianna only ever looks at home.

I should have said something else, something to get her mom to be nicer. I should have . . . maybe nothing I might have said to Brianna's mom would have mattered—or even been listened to—but I could have done more. I could have made Brianna come spend the night with me. I could have called her when I got home and double-checked to make sure she was okay.

I could stop wanting her boyfriend.

I could stop thinking about Ryan saying it was me he'd called to speak to that first time he and Brianna talked on the phone.

At home after church, I need a break from myself and my thoughts. I slide into my favorite jeans and one of Dad's old lawyer shirts, deep blue cotton that's soft against my skin and hangs loose enough for what comes next, which is Sunday breakfast, and Mom's favorite thing to cook.

Mom loves to cook, but on Sunday mornings she pulls out all the stops because Dad's favorite meal is a big breakfast and once a week she likes to "treat" him. Honestly, I sometimes wonder how he survived without Mom. I know he did—she wasn't even born until he was older than I am now, and they didn't meet until he was in his forties and she was finishing her doctoral degree, but still. It's like they've always been together and she—she really loves him and wants him to be okay. As okay as he can be.

Today she's made stuffed French toast, filling the buttery, eggy pieces of bread with a mixture of cream cheese and frozen blueberries that she'd thawed overnight, and a frittata, which is basically a huge pan full of baked eggs and cheese and vegetables. There's bacon too, and orange juice that she squeezed herself.

"Kathy, have you sent this French toast recipe in anywhere?" Dad says as he digs into his breakfast, and Mom shakes her head, pulling out her contest recipe notebook. (Of course she has one—actually, more than one. They are all over the house. And in her car.)

"Breakfast entries are usually some sort of bread or muffin," she says as she writes. "I think the next big thing will be pancakes that have been turned into some sort of layered dish. Pancake lasagna! Oh, with syrup as the sauce, and maybe chocolate hazelnut spread as the cheese . . ." She trails off and starts writing faster, in the cook-off creation zone. Dad grins and pats her non-writing hand.

"Don't forget to eat," he says, and Mom nods, absently picking up a piece of bacon and stabbing it near her mouth while still writing.

Dad starts laughing right away. I last a little while longer, but then I'm giggling too.

"Oh, hush," Mom says, grinning and finally getting the bacon to her mouth. After she swallows, she says, "Henry, how's your hip?"

"Feels better than yesterday."

Mom looks at him. "Are you going to call the doctor tomorrow?"

"For you, anything," Dad says, grinning at her, and Mom grins back, then looks at me. "I'm surprised Brianna isn't here. You two—well, you three now, I guess, since she seems to be pretty serious about Ryan—have been together a lot recently."

"Does Ryan have a friend for you?" Dad says.

"Dad! I don't—can we not discuss my social life?" Or lack thereof.

"I'm not discussing. I'm asking. Ryan seems very nice, so I thought maybe he might know someone you could—"

"Dad!" I say again, and he glances at my mother, who shakes her head at him.

"You'll meet someone," she says. "Somewhere out there is the perfect boy for you, Sarah Bear."

There is. His name is Ryan, and I can't date him because he's dating my best friend.

But I've kissed him.

"I'm full," I say, pushing away from the table. "I'm going to work on my homework."

"Don't you want to go out?"

"Mom, it's not even eleven. No one I know is up."

"Oh, of course they are," she says, as if everyone gets up at the crack of dawn on the weekends. "Why, Brianna's usually here already."

"Yeah," I mutter, and leave the kitchen, head up to my room. Mom's right. Brianna usually is here. Normally I call her when I get home from church, before I even change my clothes, and she comes over and eats with us.

But today, I didn't call her. Today I've been trying to think about her, told myself I am thinking about her, but I'm not. Not really. Not like I should.

I keep thinking about Ryan.

I keep thinking about Ryan and I haven't called her because I've wondered if he'll call me. If we'll talk about last night. Or the kiss. Or both.

I haven't called her because if I do and he's there with her, I won't be able to pretend that he might like me.

And I want to.

I want to pretend that there is a me and him. I want to pretend that the first time he called Brianna went differently than it did.

What happened the morning after that end-of-summer party was this:

Brianna was over, trying on some of Mom's lipsticks and taking them off as soon as she put one on because she didn't like any of the colors, and the phone rang. I answered it, said, "Hello?" and Ryan said, "Hi, Sarah?" and my heart pounded in my chest. I felt strangely weak but happy, leaned against the wall as Brianna peered at me and Ryan said, "Sarah?"

I said, "Ryan?" his name coming out as a squeak, and then there was silence, a painful, slow silence where I knew I had to say something but wanted him to say something because last night we'd talked and he'd touched my hand and I'd hoped but then he went off with Brianna.

With Brianna, who was smiling and smoothing her hair back even though I was the only person around. Who was motioning for me to give her the phone.

I stared at her and she whispered, "Sarah, he's called me *here*! And after I just barely mentioned that I'd probably see you today. He totally likes me."

"So, um, Sarah," Ryan said, and Brianna said, "Tell him I'm not here. No, wait, say I'm here. Oh, this is so romantic. Like, movie romantic. He called me here!" She touched the fingers of one hand to her mouth and smiled, lost in a memory, and I knew what she was thinking about.

They'd kissed. I'd seen it. They'd kissed and I'd seen him looking at her, every guy looked at her, every guy wanted her, how could they not? She was Brianna, she was beautiful. It was who she was.

"Hold on, Brianna's here," I said, and swallowed the stupid lump of hurt that clogged my throat.

And that was it. I lingered for a few moments, watching Brianna smile, hearing her laugh, and listening to her side of the conversation, "Have you been thinking about last night? Me too. What, you want to talk to Sarah now? I don't know if I can allow that. I bet you'll ask her what I said about your kissing technique, and, well, I'm afraid she doesn't have enough information to form a real opinion yet. I need more samples, you see. But Sarah did say we were perfect for each other. Yeah, she did. Listen." She grinned at me and held the phone out, waiting.

"Perfect," I said, raising my voice a little, so Ryan could hear me, and Brianna giggled and went back to talking to him. I snuck out of my own room like it wasn't mine at all and sat on the stairs trying not to cry. I thought Ryan had called me. Me.

I let myself think that once, just once, and then I forgot about it. I made myself forget it. I had to.

I had to because I watched my best friend start seeing him. I watched her start to really like him. I watched her eyes light up whenever she saw Ryan in a way they never had for any other guy. I saw them together, not for a week or even two, but for one month. Now almost two.

But now Ryan and I have kissed, and he said he wanted to talk to me when he called.

He wanted to talk to me.

The phone rings then and I jump. I wait, breathless, for someone to answer it, hear my father's voice.

I wait for him to call my name.

But he doesn't.

I finally call Brianna in the afternoon. She's getting ready to go out and says she's been screening her calls but "picked up because it's you and I heart you." I don't ask any questions, don't say, "Where are you going?" or "Who are you going out with?" I don't want to hear her answers.

"See you tomorrow?" she says, and I say, "Of course. You want to drive, or are you getting a ride with Ryan?" I don't even hesitate when I say his name.

"I'll drive," she says. "Oh, I gotta go. Fun waits!"

"Go get it," I say, and sit there after she's hung up, not thinking about anything or anyone at all. It's—it's not easy, which is weird, but I can't keep doing this, I can't keep playing "what if." I have to remember how things are.

When the phone rings after dinner, I answer, figuring it will be one of Mom's contesting friends calling so they can worry over the coming weekend, which is when the Fabulous Family Cook-Off finalist calls will go out. But it's just a wrong number, someone who hangs up as soon as they hear my voice. I try not to take it personally, but I can't help it. I'm feeling sorry for myself. I'm feeling alone.

I wish the kiss had never happened.

I wish it had never happened because then I wouldn't think about it as I'm falling asleep.

I wouldn't wake up flushed, my arms wrapped around nothing. I wouldn't be wondering what Brianna and Ryan did today.

I wouldn't be wondering if he thought of me.

eighteen

It's Tuesday night. Normally I'd be doing what I always do on Tuesday nights, which is homework, dinner, and homework.

But tonight is not normal. Tonight I am standing in front of my closet, frowning at my jeans and T-shirts, flipping through them one after the other; long sleeve, short sleeve, cute (I think), was cute (last year). I finally settle for a pair of jeans and a shirt Mom washed with a load of sheets and bleach that's now spotted in places. I like the randomness of the pattern, the mystery of how and where the bleach leached the color from the shirt.

The shoes are easy. My pink sneakers, but my hands are shaking as I tie the laces. I look at myself in the mirror. I wish I owned a padded bra. I wish I was taller.

My stomach is in knots. I barely touched my dinner, but then Dad didn't eat much of his either. The call for the Fabulous Family Cook-Off finalists will come this weekend, and Mom's can't come soon enough. Dad and I both agree on that. Even Mom does, and she's promised to stop cooking the recipes she's sent in "soon."

But now . . . now I'm supposed to go to Ryan's house. To study. With him and Brianna.

I didn't mean to be here. To be going to his house. On Monday, I rode to school with Brianna. I told myself all the Ryan stuff had to stop and made myself ask her, "What did you do last night?"

Brianna smiled and said, "Oh, you know. Stuff."

I said, "Ryan," as freely as I could, because I was trying, I really was, and she nudged her purse across the seat to me and said, "I've got this new powder in there. It'll make your nose less shiny."

I looked in the mirror of the compact in Brianna's bag. My face looked enormous, grotesque in the magnifying glow of the compact. I smoothed the puff over the powder and then my face, inhaling the smell that only expensive cosmetics have, a sort of moneyed tang.

"Much better," Brianna said, and shoved her hair back with one hand. It all fell into place neatly, swinging shining dark around her face. "Oh, look, there's Ryan."

She waved and he waved back, heading into school. He didn't look at me.

When we walked in, she steered us toward Ryan, and I kept walking because it was just Ryan, Brianna's boyfriend, and of course she had to say hi to him. That was what couples did, and I'd seen them say hi before.

I'd handed the phone to Brianna when he called my house after that party, after he and I talked. I never thought he might have been calling me.

"Hey you," Brianna said, and I looked at Ryan, planning to smile, to be normal, or try to, but when I did, I saw he was looking at me.

He was looking at me and I was back in the car with him— just like that, just that fast—whiplashed back into memory, one brief second of our mouths meeting, and then we were on the deck looking out into Brianna's backyard and he said he'd wanted to talk to me and was leaning in toward me and I wanted him closer, wanted him, and—

And I said, "I gotta go get something out of my locker," and left. Brianna called out, "See you later, Sarah!"

Ryan didn't say anything.

I saw Brianna during school, of course—she's the one person I always see, has always been the person I've waited for between classes when I could and traded smiles with in the halls when I couldn't.

She was with Ryan, and they were standing with Greg. Brianna said, "Sarah, over here," her voice lighter than usual, pleased, and so I stopped and smiled and stood there, Ryan's shoulder right next to mine while Brianna looked at Greg and talked and talked and said, "Sarah, what do you think?" Her voice was flirty.

I blinked and then said, "Madness," because that was what Brianna always wanted me to say when she sounded like that, and

I saw the curve of her smile turn toward Greg before it swung back to Ryan. Then she looped an arm through Ryan's, the couple way to walk, and waved goodbye at Greg and me, who both stood there, dazed in our own ways.

Ryan had to move to let Brianna take his arm, and I pretended I didn't feel the shiver that ran through me when his arm grazed mine. I just moved, and when I did, Ryan's eyes met mine and I saw that he remembered Friday night too. I saw he was thinking about exactly what I was. I saw he was thinking about that kiss.

I had seen that hot light in guys' eyes so many times but never at me. Not ever.

"They look happy," Greg said. I looked at him. There was a fading, mouth-shaped bruise on his neck, just the barest trace of a kiss. He was looking at Brianna.

"Almost two months," I said.

"I wish it was still Sunday," he said, and waved at me, then headed off down the hall. It was then I knew who Brianna had seen when she'd gone out, and when she came up to me after school and whispered, "We spent all of Sunday studying, okay?" I stared at her and said, "You saw Greg again?"

"Not like you think," she said. "I had to get out of the house because my mom was—well, you know. 'You'd be pretty if you lost ten pounds, or had better hair/skin/everything.' So I drove around for a while and I didn't want to do homework and I knew you'd be busy with that, and Ryan is always doing art stuff and doesn't ever want to do anything fun, just 'talk,' and Greg was hanging out in his front yard, washing his car, and so we went and got something to eat." She glanced at me. "But it was just a burger, and drive-thru even, so it's not like we were, you know, doing anything."

She waved at Ryan, who'd walked over to us, hands shoved deep into the pockets of his jeans. Brianna playfully pulled one of them free and wrapped it around her waist. "You're so quiet today. Isn't he being even more quiet than usual, Sarah?"

I shrugged, smiling at Brianna and not looking at Ryan.

I smiled and didn't look as she turned to him for a kiss. I smiled when I heard their lips meet. I smiled when Brianna said, "Bye, cute boy," and then took my hand, getting ready to tug me along to her car and then to my house where we studied and then ate dinner and Brianna said her mother had called her lawyer again and that her father still hadn't called her.

Brianna didn't cry but her voice got very quiet, and I hugged her and told her I was sorry. I meant it for what her parents were doing, I did.

But I also meant it for how I'd felt when Ryan had said, "Bye, Sarah," as me and Brianna left school. I'd turned back to look at him, startled, and he was looking at me like he had before.

So I'd said I was sorry and I was, but the sorry was for her mother, her father—and how glad I was that Ryan had looked at me like he had.

And then there was today and I avoided Brianna and Ryan. I went to the bathroom when I normally didn't go so I wouldn't see them, stood locked in a stall reading graffiti. Everyone was a slut or had a disease or should die and no one ever wrote anything nice on the bathroom walls. Not even anything hopeful.

It was like we were all so busy trying to be happy or saying we were happy, but underneath there was nothing but bitterness, the kind that could only be bled out in ink, in unspoken words.

Brianna cornered me after last period, her hair in casual, beautiful disarray. Her hands were cold, though, and frantic, clutching mine.

"You have to come with me tonight," she said. "Swear you will, Sarah. Swear," and I said, "Okay," thinking of her mother waiting for her with barbed words or her father promising something and Brianna already knowing it wouldn't happen, and how she needed me there to hold her up, to help her navigate the waters of two people who were supposed to love her.

But then she marched us down the hall to Ryan and said, "Sorry I couldn't talk last night, but I can come over tonight. Sarah needs to come too though, okay? Her mom's totally waiting to hear about the cook-off and she needs a break from that and I have to be a good friend, don't I?"

Ryan looked at her and said, "Yeah, of course," and I thought *no no no no no*. I didn't want to see him, I didn't want to be in his house.

In the car I told Brianna I couldn't go.

"You have to," she said.

"I can't."

"Why not?"

"Because I can't."

"Why?"

I sighed, wrapping my hands around my seatbelt and searching for the right words.

"Because it would be weird, okay?" I said. "I mean, you're dating him. You want to be with him, and if you're nervous about that—"

"I'm not nervous," Brianna said, her voice sharp, and then her face crumpled and she blinked hard like she only did whenever her mother was talking to her.

"He has to keep liking me," she finally said. "I don't—I don't want to be like my parents, okay? I don't want to quit when things aren't exactly how I want them to be. You get that, right?"

"Yeah, I get it, and Brianna, you aren't your parents. You *aren't*," I said, because this Brianna, scared Brianna, was one I'd never seen around a guy before, had only seen with her parents, and I wanted to fix things for her. I didn't want to see that bewildered look in her eyes.

I wanted it enough to lie to myself and think that going to Ryan's would be easy for me. That it would be nothing.

But it's not nothing.

Brianna's car isn't there when I get to his house, and I don't pull into his driveway. I drive down the street and all around the streets that branch off it in Mom's car, my hands clamped around the steering wheel because it's so much more than nothing.

I drive around until I see Brianna's car, and then I turn down his street, pretend we are both getting there at the same time.

"Why'd you come that way?" she says when we're walking toward his front door. I shrug and she says, "I was sort of hoping you'd have gotten here before me. Seen what kind of mood he's in."

"And I would—what? Report on it when you came and then leave?"

"No, you'd stay and hang out," she says, grinning at me. "You're not as boring as you think you are, you know."

"Oh," I say, and Ryan opens the door.

nineteen

I've been in Ryan's house before. Years ago, for a birthday party. I remember his mother served a cake from the grocery store, the kind with the icing that's so sweet it leaves an almost bitter taste in your mouth. I love that kind of cake, probably because Mom would never dream of bringing one into the house.

"Hey you," Brianna says to him, and wraps her arms around his shoulders, drawing him to her.

"Hey," Ryan says, kissing her forehead, and I see Brianna stiffen a little, watch her tilt her face up, rise up onto her tiptoes, and press her lips firmly against his.

I want to look away—I don't want to see them kissing even though I have no right to feel angry and sad and sick, no reason that should matter, anyway—but I don't look away. I watch

Brianna kiss him and I watch Ryan's lips brush a brief answer to her kiss before he pulls back and says, "Come on in."

"See?" Brianna says as we walk in, leaning in toward me and whispering, her hand urgent on my arm. "What was that?"

"A kiss?" I whisper back, but I know it wasn't the kind of kiss Brianna gets, and she does too, tells me, "That wasn't a kiss. The next time we go out, I'm so finding someone for you to at least make out with so we can talk about this properly because you—well, you have to know what I'm talking about."

Guilty little voice in my head: I do.

I know what a real kiss feels like.

I know what Ryan's kiss feels like.

"Maybe it's because I'm here," I say, and the minute the words are out I feel hot blood rushing to my face because I didn't mean it like that, he wasn't not really kissing her because of me.

Except that is how I meant it. How I wish it was.

"No, he's kissed me in front of you before," Brianna says, smiling at Ryan, who is heading upstairs and looking back, motioning for us to follow him. "It's just been these past couple of weeks that he's . . ." She trails off and turns away from me, turns fully to Ryan, and says, "Let's study," making it sound sexy and fun and all the things studying isn't unless you're a guy and with Brianna.

I don't want to see it. I don't want to watch them "studying" together. And yet here I am.

I follow them upstairs slowly.

Ryan's room is your typical guy's room. I only know what they look like because Brianna's told me, and from her I'm familiar with how clothes are always kept on the floor and how the curtains are almost always drawn. Ryan has all that plus an assortment of plates crusted with bits of food scattered around, but in one corner everything is neat, precisely laid out, and I see the space where he draws, sketchbooks of different sizes stacked in order, bits of paper with drawings of a leaf, a finger, and the curve of a closed eye tacked to a bulletin board.

I drift over to look at them, wishing I could open the sketchbooks. Wishing Brianna wanted to open them. But she is opening the curtains and looking out Ryan's window instead, calling him over to stand with her, pointing out a passing car and asking him what he thinks.

"I don't know," Ryan says, and Brianna says, "Come on, it's nice. Don't you think it's nice? Can't you just agree with me?"

"I don't want a new car," Ryan says, and there is something very final in his voice.

I look at Brianna, who is staring at Ryan like she has never seen him before and doesn't know what to do. It is not the frightened look she gets with her parents, but a confused look. An almost angry one. "I just said it was nice," she says, her voice coming out soft and wounded, confused. "Did I make you mad?"

"No," Ryan says, looking uncomfortable. "It's not that. It's just—"

"Good," Brianna says, and sits down on his bed, leaning back a little, her shirt parting to show the long line of her throat and the skin below it. "I guess we'd better start studying, right?" Her voice is still soft but warm now, inviting, and I fidget with the books I'm holding, slipping my fingers along their edges.

I want him to sit next to her and I want to be happy for her, but I don't want him to sit next to her, I want him to shrug and turn to me, see me looking at his pictures and cross the room to me and—

"Sarah?" Brianna says, the tiniest bit of an edge in her voice, and I shake my head and say, "Right, sorry," and hand her a chemistry textbook, sitting down on what looks like the cleanest spot on the floor. I'll be sent to get snacks or something soon enough I think, sent away so Brianna can get that alone time she wants.

"You can't study down there," Ryan says as he sits on the bed too, looking down at me as if I've done something silly.

"Oh. But you two—"

"There's room up here," he says, and pats the bed.

"Yeah," Brianna says, "tons of room," and there is room—he's got a big bed—but she doesn't sound or look pleased. I hesitate, and she says, "Come on," smiling her Brianna smile—the everything-is-great smile. Her fake smile.

I move, and so there we all are, on the bed, and I'm pretending to study and am pretty sure Brianna isn't studying at all. I see her moving around, shifting toward Ryan and trying to catch his eye.

I don't know if Ryan is studying or not. I didn't think before I sat on the bed, so I sat right next to him and I have to keep reminding myself not to look at him, not even out of the corner of my eye, but it doesn't matter.

I am so aware of how close he is, of how when he shifts on the bed his shoulder bumps against mine, and the right side of my body, the side closest to him, is thrumming, my heart beating through it, the push-pound of my blood singing just from having him so near.

"This is boring," Brianna says, and I look at her, follow her eyes to the clock, where half an hour has passed. It seems like a long time and no time at all, and I don't want things to change. And yet I desperately want them to change. It's like there's two of me.

"So what did you do on Sunday?" Ryan says to me, and I look at Brianna, who is perfectly still now, frozen.

"Studied with Brianna," I say, and the thing about the lie is that it isn't hard at all. It's easy to say, and the look of relief on Brianna's face is one I know. I'm there for her, I'm her friend, this is how things are, I've always been the person who smoothes things over for her, especially when it comes to guys.

"Of course," Ryan says, smiling at me and then Brianna, and I think of what she said. Of where she really was on Sunday. Who she was with.

And I could say what really happened, tell the truth, but I wouldn't be doing it for Ryan. I'd be doing it for me and it would hurt Brianna, make her so upset, and the scary thing is that part of me knows this and still wants to talk. Part of me doesn't care that I will be betraying her. Part of me says that she has already turned away from Ryan.

But then, hasn't he turned away too?

And I'm the one he turned to.

I know there are bigger things in the world than me, than this, that people are starving and dying and living lives that make mine look like it's gilded, and I shouldn't be so small. So petty.

I wish I didn't want Ryan so badly, but I do. I don't know how to stop it, and reminding myself that there is a whole world out past the room we're in doesn't do it. It doesn't make me a better person, it doesn't make me stop thinking about Ryan's shoulder brushing mine and how I wish for a thousand things even though I know that if they happen it will mean the end of my tiny, safe world.

"I really went over because she was upset about Tommy. You know, from the party," Brianna says, and it's the wrong thing to say but she doesn't know that. She didn't hear me and Ryan talking about it.

"Well, not really upset," I say. "I just wanted to talk to Brianna about guys and stuff."

"Don't worry, you're totally going to meet someone," Brianna says, and shoots Ryan a small smile, a see-what-I-do-to-cheer-her-up smile, and I've seen it before. I'm always the one who doesn't have a date, the one guys walk up to and say, "So, is your friend, you know, with someone?" and I may not be the only girl without someone, but it feels like it sometimes. A lot of the time.

Normally, I don't mind. I know that when I'm old, twenty-five, twenty-seven, I'll have met someone, but now I feel this rush of rage that Brianna sees me as so desperate when I have only ever wanted two guys, and both of them chose her.

But as I look at Brianna, something in me says—so quiet, like I'm afraid to hear it—*Did they?*

Did they choose her?

I called to talk to you, Sarah, I remember, and I see Brianna's hand on his arm at that first party. I see her smiling at him, a smile I know so well. That I've seen her shine on other guys.

"Sarah?" I hear, and Brianna's put one hand on my leg, tapping my knee.

"Hey," I say, and she rolls her eyes but grins at me, says, "You and your thinking."

I stare at her, watch as she gets up and walks into Ryan's bathroom, turns on the water, and comes out with one of those tiny disposable cups. She drinks from it and then turns around, tosses it back into the dark of the bathroom, but I hear it hit something, the thunk of it landing in a trash can.

She knows Ryan's room, she knows him, and I'm seeing ghosts where none live. Brianna chose to kiss Greg, she did, but Ryan chose to leave that end-of-summer party with her. He chose to sit with her. To close his eyes when she moved in to kiss him.

To kiss her back.

There is no evil villain here, no friend who is really an enemy and out to get me. Brianna goes for what she wants, but she has never taken anything that was mine.

She's never needed to. Everything came freely given, and she has done nothing but be my friend.

"Hey, I just thought of something," she says as she sits back down, plucking my knee with her fingers. "Remind me that I have some conditioner that's supposed to be great for limp hair, okay? I totally bought it for you and remembered it just now."

She looks at Ryan. "Don't you think it would help Sarah's hair?"

"She looks fine to me," Ryan says, and Brianna looks back at me and rolls her eyes.

"Guys," she says. "If you're not walking around drooling all over yourself, you look fine. I'll go grab some chips or something, okay?" She glances at Ryan again. "I know where your mom keeps everything and I could use a break from chemistry and, well, it'll—it'll be like the other night should have been."

Poor Brianna, her mother's always haunting her, and I nod to show it's a good idea. I want her to be able to replace the moment her mother ruined, I want her to be okay, and Brianna grins at me.

And then she's gone and I'm alone with Ryan.

twenty

I'm alone with Ryan. I am touching his bedspread
with one hand and quickly let go, trying not to take in the sight of
his things. Of him.

It's hard though, because he's still sitting next to me, silent but
there, and it is so quiet now. It's so quiet I can hear him breathing
and he isn't moving, I'm not moving, we are both just sitting.

It's so quiet, so silent . . . and it's a kind of silence I know. It's
one we've shared before, and it's like if either of us moves, something will happen.

"Almost ready!" Brianna calls up to us, her voice faint but
happy, and I twitch a little, startled guilty and trapped too, wanting to be here but wanting to be far away, at home as well, safe
from the thoughts racing through my head—*Ryan is here, right next*

to me, is he thinking about me, does he want to talk to me, does he want to look at me?—wanting to be safe from myself.

I should go, and that's exactly what I say to him.

"I should probably go. You and Brianna must want to be alone and—"

"No," Ryan says, and puts a hand on my arm. His fingers are warm, trembling slightly, I see them, I feel them. "I mean, can you—I want to talk to you about Friday." He lowers his voice. "I tried to call you on Sunday but I hung up because I—this—I don't—I didn't mean for all this to happen."

First thought: He remembers the kiss! He's thought about it! He is thinking about it! He called me!

Second thought: He didn't say "kissed," or "when we kissed," he didn't say exactly what happened, what we did, and I know that can't mean anything good. "About Friday" and "didn't mean" are—well, that sounds like "mistake." Plus he hung up when he called.

Two thoughts tumbling out together, giddy high to crashing low.

I wish it had just been the high.

"I didn't say anything to Brianna," I say, and I know I should look at him and smile to show I'm okay, that everything is fine, but I can't, not yet, I will just say what I need to and go. "I'm not going to, either. I know it wasn't—like you said, you didn't mean it."

"But I . . . I don't mean that I didn't mean it," he says, running a hand through his hair. "I mean, I didn't mean to kiss you, but I'm not sorry that it happened. I should be, I know, but I . . ."

He trails off and I look at him then, I can't not look at him.

"I'm not sorry," he whispers. "Not like I know I should be. I just—Sarah."

He meant it. He meant the kiss.

He wanted to kiss me.

There is red staining his face, dusting his cheekbones, his forehead, he looks nervous, but then I shift a little and we are looking at each other.

We are looking at each other and it's just us, just him and me and—

"Okay, come on down!"

And Brianna. Brianna making food and waiting for us, Brianna who wants to be with Ryan, who made me come with her because she's worried, and guilt—not like a wave, not a soft rushing, but fast and hard, a wall—slams into me.

I am here with her boyfriend talking about a kiss that would break her.

"I'm—" I say, and he says it too, we say it at the same time, two I's overlapping, echoing, and I see his face change like I know mine does, I know we are both remembering where we are. Who we both revolve around.

But the thing is—and it's horrible, I know—is that it isn't quite enough. Everything I know, and it's still not enough to make me stop thinking about Ryan as *Ryan*. It's not enough to keep me thinking of him as Brianna's Ryan, as my best friend's boyfriend.

He remembers, I remember, and we are both getting up at the same time too, getting ready to go see Brianna, and I wonder if everything in him is humming, waiting like I am, and then there we are, standing right by the door, and we can't pass through it together but we have to go through it because Brianna is downstairs, waiting.

I turn just as he does, and now we are face-to-face and I didn't turn so he could go first, I turned hoping he would turn to me and he did, he is, and there is no air in the room now, there is no air in the whole world, there is just the beat of my heart pounding fast in my chest, beating rush-hush in my ears, and he says, "Sarah," very softly.

He says my name and I look at him. He is staring at me like I am the only person in the room, the only person ever, and I shake my head because this can't be, it can't, and yet it is. I know what's going to happen.

And I want it to.

I close the space between us. I don't close my eyes. I see his face come closer, closer, and I want it to.

When he kisses me, everything stops.

I don't know how much time passes, I don't know if the universe passes us by, if it decays and dies and is born again, because everything is his mouth on mine, my mouth on his, the feel of him pressed against me, shoulders, chest, legs, and it's so much but not enough.

I want to crawl inside what's happening. I want it burned into my brain to always remember. I am stretched up on tiptoe, straining to meet him, and then he pulls me closer, hands wrapping around me, lifting me up, and he is holding me, his mouth on mine. He tastes like toothpaste, and the skin at the base of his neck is hot and smooth and he breathes faster when I press into him, brush crush of his mouth, his body, and we are pushing closer together. Can I push into him, have my heart beat with his?

"Hey, you guys, come on already," Brianna calls, her voice very close, on the stairs, and the silence, our silence, shatters.

I hear her steps and our breathing. I feel my back pressed against his door frame, I feel his hands on me, one holding my waist, the other curling lower, curved around my hip.

Breathe.

His forehead touching mine, a glimpse of his mouth.

Another kiss, we had another kiss, and I want more, so much more. I am so messed up, so—I can't stand it. I push away and grab my books. Brianna comes in then, says, "Sarah?" holding a bowl of chips in her hands, all different kinds carefully arranged and while she did that, I did this: I kissed her boyfriend.

I want her boyfriend, I forgot all about her, I forgot everything.

I shake my head, say, "I really—I have to go," and then rush downstairs, outside, wave over one shoulder when she calls after me and yell, "Yes, I'm fine, I swear I am."

I see the two of them standing in the doorway as I back down the driveway. His hands are in his pockets, his eyes impossible to see.

She is still holding the chips and starts to turn to him as I drive off, and I stare blindly at the road, trying to see it.

There are a million rules for being a girl. There are a million things you have to do to get through each day. High school has things that can trip you up, ruin you, people smile and say one thing and mean another, and you have to know all the rules, you have to know what you can and can't do.

And one of them is this: You don't kiss your best friend's boyfriend. You don't do it once. You certainly don't do it twice.

You don't because being best friends is beyond school and its quicksand of who is doing what and why, it's something stronger than that. I've known Brianna forever, she picked me to be her friend, and I've always been there for her. I've always been a good friend, and I'm not a bad person. Really, I'm not.

Except I am.

I kissed her boyfriend and then I kissed him again. We broke apart when we heard her voice, but what if we hadn't? What if she hadn't been there?

I am broken, I have cut myself wide open. I can see my heart and it is not what I believed it was, it is not good and kind and all the things I have always thought I am.

At home, I go inside and see Mom and Dad on the sofa. I watch them talking to me. I can't hear them, but I see them pointing at the phone. I see their mouths shape, "Sarah?" their faces full of concern.

I walk over to the phone, heart pounding so hard I feel sick.

"Hey," Brianna says, her voice in my ear. "Just wanted to make sure you're all right before I go. Ryan wanted to follow you home and make sure you're okay, but I said I'd call because he doesn't need to prove that he's super boyfriend. I mean, I already know that. And you are okay, right?"

"Yeah, I'm fine," I say. Just fine, I am fine, I kissed your boyfriend, I'm sorry, Brianna. "Sorry," I add, and she laughs, says, "Yeah, okay, whatever, silly." She doesn't know what I mean.

She says, "I gotta get going myself," and then click, silence, and I meant that "sorry" for the kissing but I am also sorry Ryan didn't follow me. I am sorry there wasn't—isn't—more between us. That there can't be.

This is the real unwritten rule: You don't want what you know you shouldn't. And I haven't just broken that rule. I have wrecked it, smashed it, and still . . .

And still I want.

twenty-one

I go up to my room, dazed, and sit on my bed. I press my fingertips to my closed eyes, like I can push away what I see. Push away what happened.

I'm never going to fall asleep. I try anyway. I get ready for bed; put on pajamas, brush my teeth. Sit in bed with the light on, staring at nothing.

I lie down and close my eyes. I open them again right away because, of course, Ryan is who I see.

Eventually I give up trying to sleep. I sit up and flick on the light by my bed, then thumb through the magazines I have stacked on the floor. I never read the articles, because they are always the same—Believe in yourself! Also, here's how to have better skin and lose weight!—but sometimes the pictures give me sneaker ideas.

And right now I need an idea. A distraction.

The magazine I pick up is a fat one, bloated with pictures of what's new, except they call it "fresh," and I cover up the tall heels on a picture of a model leaping.

For her I would pick a pair of old canvas high-tops, like the kind basketball players used to wear, and I would turn the laces the other way, put the bow at the toes, and fill in the bits of worn fabric with buttons glued to almost close the gap, leave just enough space for a hint of sock (striped, I think) to show through.

I like the button idea, and the bow at the bottom of the shoe too, but I can't do anything with it, can't *see* it. I've been doing all of this, playing at being myself, at being normal, but the whole time my mind has spit images at me, tonight at Ryan's replaying a thousand times, a never-ending loop that's got me sitting here worrying. Wondering.

Remembering us kissing.

I will push it all away in a moment, I want just one last moment.

And then I remember seeing Brianna kiss Ryan at that party. End of the summer, my mind shrieking in angry hurt even though I had no reason to be angry. Ryan wasn't mine, and he clearly wanted to be hers.

He *is* hers.

I push the magazine off the bed and try to chase away the thought that comes up right behind it.

This one: Maybe he could be yours. She's kissing someone else, after all. Why shouldn't he kiss you?

I wish I had told her no tonight when she asked me to come with her. I don't say it to Brianna very often, but if I had, I wouldn't be awake right now having a silent debate with myself over exactly how wrong kissing Ryan is, with Very Wrong! making its case and But Remember How It Felt! making its point at the same time.

I grab a pair of blank shoes, plain white canvas, and look at them, try to decide what I should do with them. I trace a finger over them, trying to imagine a design.

I'm tracing cubes.

Cubes, like Ryan has seen me draw, like we talked about the night—

Okay, stop. I'm not thinking about that. I won't.

Start simple. What color should they be?

Blank. I can't see a color, I can't see anything but tonight, the kiss, and I can't stop seeing it.

I don't want to.

I wish someone would come and tell me what to do, tell me how to make everything work out, but there's nothing, just night and silence and my own tangled thoughts.

twenty-two

The next morning, Ryan shows up at my house.
He tells my parents we are lab partners and we end up in my room
sitting next to each other, so quiet, so tensely quiet, and then we
are kissing and he says he can't live without me, that he has to be
with me, and that Brianna already knows, he talked to her last
night and she's happy for us, she wants us both to be happy
because I'm her best friend and—

Oh, forget it.

What really happens is that I eat oatmeal and get ready for
school. Ryan doesn't show up, and even if he had, I couldn't even
think of a way for my stupid fantasy to end happily ever after.

Brianna comes to get me, says, "Ryan was so sweet to me last
night," on our way to school. "He walked me to my car and said

he really cared about me and that we needed to talk, and I wished I didn't have to go, but with Mom these days, I don't want to . . . well, you know. It sucked but it did remind me of what I love best about him, and that's how when he says stuff—like how much he cares—you know he means it."

Love. She said *love*.

She never says that about guys, not ever, but she's said it now.

"Of course he cares, it's you," I say, but my words come out hoarse, sad, and she says, "Sarah, there's a guy out there for you, I know there is. You should think about a freshman, you know? For fun. You could maybe get one of them to go out with you."

"Yeah, maybe." Maybe I could get a freshman. Maybe. I slump in my seat and Brianna smiles and sings along with the songs she's playing.

Right now, I hate my life way more than I hate me.

I wait for the guilt to kick in, for all the stuff I'm carrying—and it is like I'm carrying something, like there's this weight pressing on me, one that I hate but welcome at the same time, and who feels stuff like this? Who doesn't know the right thing to do is the right thing to do and just does it?

I think of Mom and Dad and how happy they are and press my hands together. Maybe if I focus on being here, in the car with Brianna, instead of always thinking, always wishing and wondering, things won't be so bad.

And they aren't. Or at least, I don't think they are until I'm about halfway through the day and see Brianna heading toward me with Ryan behind her, the fingers of one of her hands linked through his.

She waves at me and says something, but I can't hear it over the roaring in my ears, all the blood in my body rushing to my head, where it beats behind my eyes, a pinching pain worse than tears.

It's not seeing Brianna and Ryan together that's doing it. It's how Ryan looks at me.

How he doesn't.

The whole time Brianna talks, and she is talking, I know it, I see her mouth move, I watch him out of the corner of my eye.

He never looks at me.

"So I reminded him we don't have assigned seating," Brianna says, bumping my shoulder with hers as she leans in closer, and I make myself focus, make myself listen. "And then he said, 'Brianna, you can't sit wherever you want,' and I was like, 'Well, you should have said we actually have assigned seats.'"

"Which you don't."

"Right," Brianna says, and Ryan pulls away from her, his expression strained, still not looking at me as he mutters, "I gotta go," and walks off.

Brianna says, "Okay, Mr. Tense," laughter in her voice and a smile on her face, but for a second—just a moment, just the blink of an eye—she looks furious and somehow lost. And then she's smiling again, grinning at Greg as he walks by and pretends he can only get past us by running a hand along her back. He winks at me, turning enough to plant a quick kiss on top of my head.

"Perv," Brianna calls after him, and then looks at me. "I think he likes you."

"Greg?"

"Is anyone else kissing you?"

I freeze, but there's nothing angry in her voice, no knowledge, just teasing, and I shake my head. No. No, no one else is kissing me. "Greg still likes you."

"No, he did like me," Brianna says. "But we're over. So over."

I shrug and glance at her neck. She must see where I'm looking because she puts a hand there and then quickly moves it away. "You know that what happened with Greg didn't mean anything, right? It was just a couple of moments."

"Yeah," I say, because I do. I understand what a moment is all too well now, and I just have to get through today and the next and . . . I close my eyes and wish for strength. For something, anything to get me through this.

Here's what I get: When I come out of sixth period, Ryan is there, walking by my class when I know this isn't where he's supposed to be. I see him and he smiles, not like he normally does, but with a tense, hesitant curve of his mouth, a not-smile that extends up to his eyes, which are looking all around me. But still not at me.

"Hey," he says, falling into step beside me, and I know Ryan. He's not a new, mysterious guy I can't read. He's Ryan, and Ryan doesn't talk an awful lot. He also doesn't come up to you for no reason, and the last time I saw him smile at me like he just did was the day after he and Brianna talked on the phone at my house.

The day after the call—and the night after bowling—she and I got to school and he was there. We walked toward him and he had this strange, tense smile on his face, like he didn't know what to do or say and I thought—just for a second—of how I could talk to him when Brianna turned away, but she didn't, she went right up to him and said, "Hey you." She said that and so I turned away instead.

"I—can we talk for a second?" he says now, and I slow down. We slow down, squeeze into a corner of space, people going by around us, but all I can see is him. "Last night, you and me—what happened, it's—see, Brianna is sweet, and Sarah, I really—"

"You're sorry," I say, and I know the words come out strangely, fast so I won't have to hear him say more. Not because I don't want to but because I do, and it just—

He likes me enough to kiss me. I know that. I even think he might like me more than that, I think he might not be sorry about the kiss at all. But like he said, Brianna is sweet.

Brianna is also my best friend and I don't want to hurt her. I don't want to be that girl, the one who breaks the unwritten rule. At least, not more than I've already broken it.

So I say, "Hey, look—don't worry about it. It's forgotten."

"Forgotten?"

"Shazam!" I say stupidly—so stupidly, but I want to get away because knowing what to do doesn't mean it doesn't hurt—and he blinks. Stares.

"Like magic, you know?" I say. "Anyway, it's gone, just like that," and oh please, let me stop talking, let me not have just said "Shazam!" like I'm six or an idiot or both, but I've said it, it's out there.

I've said it's gone. That it's forgotten. I've done what I'm supposed to do.

"I need to get to class," I say, and head down the hall, probably walking too fast, and make myself slow down. Walk like I'm fine. And I am, sort of. This was the right thing and I'm not going to cry. My eyes aren't burning, I am blinking hard because I am thinking and not because I am stupid and sad.

After school, I find Greg, who looks surprised to see me but is happy to walk me to Brianna's car and slings an arm around me as we get there, just in time for Brianna to see us.

"What's up with you two?" she says, and Greg says, "Wouldn't you like to know?" waving the fingers of the arm wrapped around my shoulders at Brianna, who laughs and says, "You wish. Sarah, we gotta get out of here, okay? Greg, bye. BYE."

I pull away, Greg calling out, "What, no kiss?" to her, to me—does it matter?—and then we are in Brianna's car and she says, "Was he bothering you?"

"No," I say. "He doesn't bother me at all."

"Okay, good. Are you sure, though? Because he had his arm around you and stuff."

"It didn't mean anything."

"I know that," she says. "I mean, I think maybe it could, but it doesn't yet, and I don't want you to get your hopes up and stuff, you know? I don't want you to get hurt."

"Don't worry," I say, looking down at my hands clenched tight in my lap. I force them free, force them to relax. "He can't hurt me."

twenty-three

I want to be alone, but I'm not, Brianna comes
over, comes inside my house with me. She almost always comes
over after school and she always walks into my house like it's her
own. Normally, I like that, but not—

Not today.

"Brianna," I say as we're putting our bags down. "I have a lot
of homework and I need to focus, you know?"

"You work too hard already," she says. "You've got huge circles
under your eyes. But don't worry, they don't look that bad."

She glances toward the kitchen and calls out, "Do I smell
food?"

"You do," Mom calls back. "I've been working on recipes all
day. Hungry?"

"Starved," Brianna says, and we end up sitting in the kitchen. Brianna tries each of the three kinds of pasta salad Mom has made and offers up loads of comments. ("I like the bacon in this one." "Oooh! The sauce is great in this!")

"You like it?" Mom says, smiling at Brianna. "I started with a vinaigrette, but then thought, why not add a little cayenne for kick? I don't think you can taste that, though. I still need a little something more." She looks at me. "Sarah, honey, how was your day?"

"She says she has homework, but she always says that," Brianna says. "Oh! But there's a guy at school who likes her."

"Really?" Mom says, and I shake my head.

"He doesn't. He's just—he's all huggy and stuff."

"Huggy?" Brianna says, giggling. "Greg isn't huggy. He put his arm around you. I'm going to ask him if he wants to go out with you. Then you and him and me and Ryan can go out."

"I don't know. I—"

"Come on, it'll be fun," Brianna says. "We can make them take us out to dinner somewhere nice. I have the cutest dress, and we'll go out and get you something fantastic to make you look way different. Sexy . . ." She glances at Mom. "But not too sexy, of course."

Mom starts picking up the plates. "Sarah, you've got a dentist appointment in about twenty minutes. Brianna, do you want me to wrap you up a little something to take home?"

"No, I'm fine," Brianna says, and gives my mom a hug before she tugs me up from the table and we head back toward the front door.

"I wish we could hang out more now," she says. "I feel like

today was sort of weird or something. Do you feel like that?"

Yes. But I shake my head no.

She squints at me. "Are you sure Greg didn't ask you out? Because he really looked like he was."

"He didn't."

"You'd tell me if he did, right? I mean, not that I'd care, but we were together for a little while and it might be sort of weird. Plus he—I don't know. He doesn't really seem like your type."

"You're right," I say, my voice tight. "He's not. And besides, I think he's still into you."

"Oh, that's just how he is," she says, hugs me, and then goes.

I head back into the kitchen. "Dentist appointment? Since when?"

Mom doesn't look up from the pot she's stirring. "Sarah, I— well, you know I like Brianna, but sometimes she . . . sometimes I wish she talked to you a little differently. More nicely."

Mom has said this before. Not a lot, but she has said it, and I sigh, not wanting to argue with her. "She's my best friend, Mom."

"I know, and you've been friends for a long, long time. But she has this way of putting you down that I don't really like, and I also think that sometimes Brianna takes advantage of how kind you are."

I look away from Mom. "I'm not kind."

"Of course you are."

"I'm not," I say, and head to my room, thinking of things I've done. And how I haven't said anything about them. How I'm not sorry like I should be.

When Brianna calls that night, I tell Mom I have a headache.

She gives me one of those Mom looks, the I-see-you've-been-thinking-about-what-I-said one, and then tries to talk to me before I go to bed.

"I'm really tired," I tell her, and close my eyes.

"You know you can tell me anything," she says.

Not this. Definitely not this. But I nod like I can, then say good night and close my eyes. I keep them closed until I hear her leave.

I'm still awake when my parents go to bed. The two of them have been together for twenty years, forever, and I wonder how they do it. If they think about their pasts, the time before they were together. If there are things they wish they'd done differently. If there are things they still long for, things they wanted that never came to be.

twenty-four

It's Thursday morning, and I've decided I can't go to school. I just can't. Last Friday, seven days ago today, I went to a party with Brianna and Ryan and then got a ride home with Ryan.

Seven days ago, Ryan and I kissed. And then, two days ago, we kissed again, and then yesterday—

Yesterday I said what I needed to.

And it sucked. It sucked so much and I can't do it today, can't smile when I see Brianna and Ryan, can't see them and—

No, I need a break today.

I lie in bed until Mom comes to see why I'm not up.

"I'm sick," I say, and I don't have to fake the shakiness of my voice. Or the way I want to hunch in a ball, like I'm in pain.

I think having a stupid heart is pretty damn painful, even if the pain isn't physical.

"What's wrong?" Mom says, feeling my forehead with the back of her hand and then peering down at me. "You don't feel warm."

"My stomach," I say, and curl up tighter. "Can you call Brianna for me and tell her not to come get me?"

"All right," Mom says quietly, and I hear her on the phone to Brianna a minute later.

She doesn't say anything after that, but I can tell she wants to and so I close my eyes, curl up, and pretend I'm asleep.

After a while, Mom wants me to take something for my stomach and I do because it hurts now.

It hurts because I know Brianna will wonder what's wrong with me. I don't not talk to her, not ever. Even when I had the flu last Christmas, I talked to her when she called, let her come over and hang out while I shivered and ached all over and she pretended she didn't care that her mother had gone out to eat with "a friend" on Christmas Day and had given her a bunch of exercise DVDs and a diet book as her "gift."

Dad comes in then, dressed in his work clothes and ready for his first, late-morning class. He used to wear neatly pressed suits and crisp, starched shirts. Now he wears wrinkly pants and one of his old white work shirts. It's wrinkled too, and there's a big ink blot on the right cuff.

"Not feeling so good, I hear," he says, and sits on my bed. "Your mother says it's a stomach thing."

I nod and he touches my hair.

"Your mother also said she called Brianna and told her you

didn't need a ride and that you didn't talk to Brianna when she called last night," he says, and I glance at him.

"Did you two have a fight?" he says, and I shake my head because we didn't, we haven't, but if she knew—

If she knew what I'd done, she'd hate me. If I even told her how I feel—my eyes fill with tears.

I'm an idiot. Why can't I want someone else?

"Sarah Bear, don't cry," Dad says. "I know things seem bad now, but friends have fights, and you two have known each other forever. You just be the wonderful girl you are and everything will be fine."

It won't, I want to scream. How can it? But I just say, "Thanks, Dad."

He nods. "No problem. Everyone deserves a day off once in a while. Though you will be going to school tomorrow, right?"

"Right," I say, because his question isn't really a question, it's one of those yes-you-will parent things. Plus staying home for a thousand years couldn't cure what's really wrong with me.

Well, I guess it would, because I'd be dead, but even then my dying thought would be about Ryan, about how he looked at me in the car and in his house before we kissed, how his mouth felt on mine each time, how amazing both kisses—

Crap. Crap crap crap crap crap.

Think about something else. Something awful.

Like what Brianna would say if I told her that I'd kissed Ryan not once, but twice.

I know what she'd do. Her face would get that chilly blank look she learned from her mother and she would say, "What do you mean, 'kissed'?" and I would tell her everything, I would bleed out the details and she would just stare at me and then never talk to me again.

That works. It pushes the kisses back, and when Mom finally lets me out of bed, I eat what she's made me for lunch and then lie on the sofa, flipping through the channels and stopping at the movie I somehow knew would be on.

It's Brianna's favorite, and I watch the girl get the guy and smile at the clumsy but nice best friend. I don't wonder about the rest of the best friend's life, the part that isn't shown. She doesn't need to be a spy or an assassin. She's just who she is, a nice, supportive person. That's enough, right?

Not for me, not now, and I decide I need a cause to believe in. Something to fill the space in my heart that Ryan has written all over. Something noble, like fighting a disease. I could write letters or design a pair of sneakers and sell them to raise money. Or better yet, I could do both and maybe end up famous, which would be great.

At the very least, I'd have something really good to put on my college applications.

Yes, that's what I'll do. I'll be "cause girl." I won't even think about guys. I'll be too busy, and even in college I'll be so committed to my cause that I won't have time for anyone, but one day I'll be talking about what I believe in and there will be this guy there.

There will be a guy and he'll come up to me afterward and tell me that what I said was amazing. He'll be smart, and his dark hair will flop around his face, and his eyes will be so blue I'll feel like I'm looking at the sky, and he'll say, "Sarah, you don't know how long I've wanted to talk to you like this. I've always thought you were amazing and now that we're here, together, I think it's a sign," and I'll say, "A sign? Ryan, you had me at amazing," and he'll grin and lean in and—

And it's come back to him. To Ryan.

I bury my face in the sofa and listen to Mom moving around in the kitchen, humming under her breath as the phone rings. I wonder if I should look into voodoo or spells or if I can somehow fall into a world where faeries or dragons or both exist. If I was somewhere like that, I'd have to work with the faeries or dragons or whatever—or maybe battle them. Either way, it would be something huge, something life-changing.

Something to stop me from thinking about Ryan.

"Sarah, phone," Mom says, and I glance at the clock. I see school is out, and know it's Brianna.

I'm not going to find any spells or get sucked into another world or anything like that. I just have to—I just have to be who I'm supposed to be. I'm Brianna's best friend. I listen to her. I'm happy for her.

Well, I'm not that happy now. But I'll fake it until it's real and things are normal again.

"Hey you," I say, picking up the phone, waiting for Brianna's voice to fill my ear.

"Hey," Ryan says.

twenty-five

"Ryan?" I say, and my voice rises, his name coming out as an almost squeak. "I didn't—you're calling me?"

"You weren't in school," he says. "And I—well, I wanted to make sure you're okay. Are you okay?"

I sit up on the sofa, shaking with shock and exhilaration. "I'm . . . I'm fine. I just—" Great. What are you going to say now, Sarah? "I needed to spend a day forgetting about you, and oh, by the way, it isn't working. And hey, how about those two kisses. I can't forget them and I'm not even sure I'll ever be able to look at you normally again, despite the whole 'Shazam!' thing."

Oh yes, why don't I try that?

"I just needed some rest," I finally say. "Drink lots of fluids, that kind of thing." Oh, even better! Think brain, think! "Um.

What are you doing now? I mean, besides talking to me."

Relatively normal. I guess. I hold my breath, wondering what he'll say.

He's silent for a moment, and then says, "Well, I started working on a sketch of that abandoned house out by where they're putting in that new road. Have you seen it?"

I nod, and then remember he can't see me.

"I have. It's very . . ." I trail off, trying to think of something positive to say about the house and then remember I'm not trying to get him to like me. I've made plans to be a big innovator! Or something. And to not want him.

"It's so run-down," I say. "So sad looking. But an angry kind of sad."

"Exactly," he says, and he sounds so happy I grin and squirm on the sofa, totally forgetting all the things I just told myself. "I look at it and think about ghost stories. You know how the ghosts in them are always sad or angry or waiting for something? It got me thinking, what if ghosts are just there? Like, they have nowhere else to go. I want to try and capture that, the sense of hopelessness. I'm thinking of going out there on Sunday and looking at it again because so far, the sketches I've done are missing something."

I smile. He's so . . . well, Ryan. "So, spending your Sunday looking at an abandoned house? Don't you know you're supposed to be out having corrupting experiences?"

"Well, I was going to sit in my basement, get really drunk and brood about life, and then go start a fire or two."

"That's more like it. But I think you have to write poetry before you can move on to starting fires."

He laughs. "Do you ever wonder if people really know what they're supposed to do? Is there a moment where you just know what you're supposed to do forever?"

"My dad says it's when you finish college and get your first student loan statement," I say. "But he and my mom both went right back for more school, so I don't know if they're trustworthy. I mean, college is okay. But the last thing I want to do after sixteen straight years of school is even more school."

"So, you want to get a job," Ryan says. "What do you want to do?"

"Um . . ."

"I hate that question so much," he says, laughter in his voice, and I say, "Thank you! My parents don't really bother me about it too much, but at school all you hear is how you have to think about the future, like I have to plan every class I'm going to take in college right now and it's like, 'Hi, can I maybe try to get through chemistry first?'"

"Or the SATs."

"Ugh, don't remind me. How weird is it that one test—?"

"Matters so much to colleges?" he says. "I know. I don't get it. I keep thinking about how all my stuff will go in front of some admissions person and they'll look at my pictures and my grades and my test scores, and that will supposedly say how well I'll fit in or achieve or whatever. It's like paper matters, not me."

"Art programs want SAT scores too?"

"Everyone wants them. I bet even sneaker design programs want them."

"If only," I say. "I thought about design for a while, but I don't want to make clothes. Plus, after watching the last season of *Design You*—forget it. I'm so not interested in having to try and make something out of foil."

"What, you didn't like the poncho with wraparound leggings?"

"It was beyond hideou—wait a minute. You watch that show?"

"My mom loves it."

"But you're supposed to be sulking in the basement getting ready to light fires."

"What can I say? I'm a failure as a teenager. I watch TV with my mom."

"And spend your Sundays looking at old houses."

"That too. Want to come?"

"You . . . really?"

"Yeah." His voice sounds different now, softer and more unsure.

I can see it now, the two of us sitting on the grass outside the old house talking about art and life and how in the world we're supposed to figure out the rest of our lives right now, and he'll smile at me and I'll smile back and we'll just know we can kiss and then—

And then Brianna will say, "This is so boring. Can't we go look at something that isn't falling down?"

I swallow hard. "Brianna won't want to go."

"Yeah, but I—" He breaks off and then blows out a breath. "Sarah, look, about yesterday, at school, what I wanted to say was that I wish I—that party over the summer, the one I asked you if you remembered—do you remember it?"

My heart starts pounding really hard. "Yes." My voice is barely a whisper.

"Me too," he says, and his voice is quiet too. "I wish . . . Sarah, I wanted to keep talking to you, but Brianna was so—"

"Beautiful."

"No," he says. "She was so sure. She just came right out and said she liked me. No one had ever said that to me before and it was . . . it was so easy with her. I knew she liked me and when I talked to you, I didn't know what was going to happen. And it was—I don't know." He falls silent for a moment.

"It was terrifying," he finally says. "I didn't know if you liked me, if what I felt was what you felt too. But I wanted to know, and I figured Brianna was done with me anyway, so I called you the next day because I wanted to ask you out and then Brianna got on the phone and you—you acted like nothing had happened with us. And I guess nothing did, because really, we just talked, but I wanted—I wanted more."

"But you and Brianna, you're . . . you're happy," I say, and even as I say it, I think back over the past few weeks, over how Brianna has been so worried about Ryan, about how he doesn't act like every other guy she's been with, how he's been saying they need to talk and then she—

Then she started bringing me along with her. How she left right after I did last night. How she's always so careful not to be alone with Ryan for too long.

Even when I went over to her house with her laundry, a little over a week before Ryan and I kissed for the first time, he said he'd come over to talk to her. And she'd made it so he had no chance to.

"We—we don't work," Ryan says. "Sarah, I can't—I have to say this, okay? Just . . . please let me say it."

"Okay," I say, heart pounding even harder now.

"We kissed last Friday. We kissed on Tuesday. And even before that, I wanted—Sarah, I've wanted to kiss you. I want to kiss you again. I want—I want to go out with you."

Me. He wants me. He wants to be with me.

Me!

"I—are you sure?"

"Yeah," he says. "I'm sure. Brianna isn't . . . she's not right for me. She's not you. I'm talking to her tonight no matter what. I'm going over to her house and telling her it's over because I have to. I don't want to lie about how I feel anymore. I want to be with you, and Brianna should be with someone who wants to be with her. It's not—it's not right for me to see her when all I do is think about you."

"Oh," I say, because most of my brain has gone off line, tangled up in knowing he's been thinking about me. That he wants me.

That he's going to break up with Brianna. Tonight.

I hear a car coming up the driveway, probably Dad coming home, and maybe he'll let me borrow his car, which is way nicer than Mom's, and it'll be me and Ryan snug inside it on Sunday.

Sunday can happen now. Him and me, just us, and we'll be together, and Brianna—

And I don't hear the garage door opening. I hear a car door slam.

I stand up, look out the window.

I see Brianna's car in the driveway.

I see Brianna, here.

"Sarah?" Ryan says, and I could give the phone to Brianna now, could say, "Hey, Ryan wants to talk to you." I'd talk to Brianna afterward, I would, I'd be there for her, and it can all work out, this can really happen, me and Ryan can be together and—

And the problem isn't that I don't believe him. I do believe him. I believe he wants to be with me. I feel it in my heart, which I know sounds stupid, but I do and it's amazing.

The problem is that this will hurt Brianna. Ryan could break up with her right now and even if he didn't say it was because of me, she isn't stupid. She would figure it out. She wouldn't see him staring longingly at her when he was talking to me, and that never happens. She'd know, and would she be happy then?

I don't think so.

The problem is that I want to be with him, but there is no way to do it without hurting her, and right now Brianna is walking up my front steps, blinking hard, her eyes red and swollen even as tears stream down her face.

Brianna doesn't cry much, but she does when things with her parents are bad. And now she's here, and I know something's happened with them. I know she needs a friend. I know she needs me.

"I have to go," I tell Ryan. "Don't—don't do anything yet. Brianna's here, and she's upset. I have to talk to her."

"Her parents?" he says, and I feel a little twinge that he knows her so well.

"I'm pretty sure."

"I hope she's okay," he says, and then pauses for a second. "But Sarah, I still—I have to talk to her. I know who I want to be with, and it isn't her."

I grip the phone so tight I feel it digging into my hand, and only have time to whisper, "Ryan," before the doorbell rings and I have to hang up.

I have to because if I don't, I will shatter. I am caught in a huge tangle I don't know how to get out of. I want Ryan, but I don't want to lose Brianna.

I open the door. Maybe it really can all work out. People have been to the moon and cured diseases and found ways to inject cream into snack cakes.

But that stuff doesn't involve love. Or how you have to open the door to your crying best friend and know that you love her, you want to be there for her—but that you've done something that would make her cry too.

twenty-six

"I just saw my dad," Brianna says. We're standing in the front hallway, and she's crying so hard the words come out jagged.

"What happened?" I say, and Mom comes out of the kitchen, her recipe notebook in one hand, a distracted look on her face. It fades as soon as she sees Brianna.

"Brianna, honey, what's wrong?" she says, and Brianna walks over to Mom and hugs her. She's tall enough that she has to scrunch her head down to rest it on Mom's shoulder, but she does and Mom looks at me. Her eyes are wide but not with surprise. With sadness. She knows—just like I do—that there's only one thing that can make Brianna break like this.

Brianna lets out a long, shuddering sigh, her tears quieting, but keeps leaning into Mom.

"I don't understand them," she says. "Why don't they love me?"

"Oh, Brianna, they do," Mom says, giving her a quick hug. "They just have so much anger between them that you're caught in it."

"You think?"

"Absolutely," Mom says, and her gaze flickers to me, uneasy. We both know she is lying. And we both know that she has to because the truth is too awful to say.

"Thanks," Brianna says, pulling away from Mom, and from the look on her face, she knows it's a lie too. "Sorry about crying all over you."

Mom shakes her head. "Don't apologize. You know you're always welcome here, although today I'm afraid you might catch Sarah's cold."

"Oh yeah, that," Brianna says, stepping away from Mom and standing like she usually does, confident and smiling, eyes bright even though they're still tinged with red. "How are you?"

"She was just lying down in the living room talking to some-one on the phone when you came," Mom says. "Who was it, Sarah Bear?"

"I wasn't on the phone," I say. I hate lying to Mom but I have to do it now.

"But I heard . . ." Mom says, and trails off, her expression going thoughtful for a moment. "Well, I thought I heard you talking. But I guess it was the TV." She glances at Brianna. "You know how I get when I'm working on a recipe. In one ear, right out the other. Can I get you something to drink or eat?"

Brianna shakes her head and looks at me. I know that look, the we-need-to-talk look, and so I say, "Mom, we're going to go upstairs, okay?"

Mom nods and pats Brianna's arm again. She gives me a look, a fast one, as she heads back to the kitchen, and I can tell she knows I was on the phone. I just can't tell if she knows who with.

As we head up to my room, Brianna says, "I was surprised you didn't call me this morning. I even . . . I actually got kind of mad. But now I wish I hadn't because you're sick and I—I'm sorry, Sarah."

"It's okay," I say, walking into my room and sitting down on my still unmade bed. I do feel sick now, because Brianna is clearly upset and yet is being nice to me, telling me she's sorry and feeling my forehead with the back of her hand, like Mom does when she's checking to see if I have a fever.

"You don't feel warm," she says. "Not that I really know what I'm doing. You want some water or something?"

I shake my head but she gets me some anyway, and I think about what Ryan said, that he'll talk to her tonight, that he'll end it, and how I started thinking about me and him being together.

How I didn't think about her at all.

I can do it now, though.

"Brianna," I say when she comes back, taking the water she gives me and putting it on my nightstand. "What happened to you?"

"I—I went to see Dad at work," she says. "I skipped last period to go but he was busy, of course, like he always is, so I had to wait. I felt so stupid sitting there, but then I finally got to go back to his office. And when I did, he said he was surprised to see me and I said, 'What, not surprised and happy?' and he said—he said—" She breaks off and looks down at her hands, which are clenched into fists.

"He said he was done," she finally says, the words coming out in a sob, and at first I think I've heard her wrong.

"Done?"

"Yeah. He said he's done with me. He's going to make some sort of final settlement or something with Mom. Give her everything she wants plus more in return for her promise that all the custody stuff—and that's how he said it, 'custody stuff,' like I'm not even a person—is done. And I thought . . . I actually thought that was good."

She sniffs. "I even said that. I said, 'It'll be over then, and we can see each other all the time.' I even started talking about his new apartment and how I wish I could have seen it when he got it but it'd be great to see it now, and he looked at me. He just looked at me like—I don't know. And then he said, 'No.'"

"No?"

"Yeah," she says. "Just like that. 'No,' he says. 'I can't do this anymore. The court battles, the visitation games, I can't do any of it.' And I said, 'Right, and now it'll be over,' and he said, 'Yes, and when you're older, maybe we can see each other again, but now, whenever I see your mother or you, I realize my life . . .'" She balls her hands into fists and presses them to her eyes.

"He says we've made his life toxic. Poisoned it. That's what he said. 'I realize my life is toxic,' and I said, 'But that's Mom, not me,' and he said, 'I'm sorry, I can't help it. Whenever I look at you, I see her, and everything feels poisoned.'" She starts to laugh but it isn't a laugh at all, it's a harsh wracking sound of anger. Of grief.

"He did say he was sorry, though," she says, her voice broken. Bitter. "He told me he's doing whatever it takes to get rid of me, but hey, he's sorry, and maybe he'll see me in a few years."

"He can't really mean it."

"He does. He's gone. Like, forever gone. And he's my dad! How can he leave me like this?"

I hug her because there isn't anything to say.

There is no answer to her question. It's one that shouldn't ever be asked. But Brianna's had to do it. She's had to ask it.

And the unfairness of the answer she got—what words could ever make that better?

twenty-seven

"Do you think he'll ever get in touch with me again?"
Brianna says after a little while, her tears slowing.

"I—" I start to say, but she cuts me off.

"No, wait, don't answer that. Let's face it, we both know what
the answer is. He won't." She leans across my bed and grabs my
phone.

"Are you calling him?" I ask, wondering what will happen if
she does.

She shakes her head, dialing, and then tucks the phone under
her ear.

"Hey, Ryan." Her voice cracks as she says his name, and
then she is telling him what happened and she is crying again,
sobbing so hard she starts to choke, and then she drops the

phone, says, "Talk to him, Sarah. Tell him the rest of it."

"Brianna—" I can't talk to Ryan now. I don't want to be in this place I'm in, where I feel so bad for her that I hate what I've done, hate myself and want to pretend it all away, but she's still crying so hard, says, "Please. I can't—I don't want to say the end of it again."

I pick up the phone.

"Brianna?" Ryan says. "Brianna, are you there?"

"No," I say, and my voice is shaking. "It's Sarah. Brianna can't—she can't talk anymore right now. She's really upset."

"What's wrong with her dad?" Ryan says, sounding concerned, and I know he is. He cares, he's nice, that's one of the things I love about him, that—

That I *love* about him.

No, wait. I can't love him, not now, not like this, but I—

But I do.

"Sarah?" he says, and I can tell this is hurting him, that he feels bad for Brianna even though he cares about me. He has a soul that shines.

And me—if you could see mine now there would be a stain on it, it would be nothing but a dark fog because I know it's good that he cares about Brianna, that he's a nice guy, but I want him to care about me, just me. It's *awful*. That's the only word for it, for me, and yet I still want it to be just him and me.

I want that, but things aren't simple and there isn't a just him and me. There's him and me and Brianna.

"Sarah," Ryan says again. "I wish—"

"Yes," I let myself say once, just this once, because I do wish,

I have wished, and now I know Ryan does too, which makes things better.

And so much worse.

"Here, I can talk now," Brianna says, startling me—and then motions for me to hand her the phone.

I do, and she says, "Sarah's just being protective. I'm okay, really. Well, mostly."

I stare at her, and she stares back at me, smiling her easy, everyday grin, her Brianna smile. It doesn't quite reach her eyes, though.

"No, I don't want—I need to be alone tonight," she says. "You don't have to come over. No, really, please don't. Besides, we're going out tomorrow. So I'll just see you at school, okay? Bye."

She hangs up the phone and turns to me, says, "I know I said I couldn't talk, but you were looking all super intense and didn't really talk, which was what you were supposed to do, remember? So I worried you'd freak him out, and you can't do that with guys. I mean, look at my dad. He'd rather never see me than put up with my mother's crap. And that's not going to happen with Ryan."

I swallow. "He's not the kind of guy who'd get upset because you're hurting."

"You don't know him like I do."

"I've known him forever, Brianna. We both have, remember?"

She frowns. "Okay, we have. What's wrong with you? I'm the one whose dad was just a total jerk, remember?" She sighs and leans off my bed, flicking at my magazines. "I can't—I need to not talk about this or think about it, okay?"

"I—you're right," I say. "Things have been a little intense. I've been a little intense." I take a deep breath. I will do this. I will do what I know I should, and I will tell her everything. I will tell her I like Ryan. I'll tell her I kissed him. I'll tell her I know he's her boyfriend and that I will do anything—*anything*—to make it up to her. "I—the thing is, I—"

"Oh, I get it," she says, sitting back up and smiling a little. "I knew you were acting weird downstairs, and now I totally know why."

What? How? I thought I wanted to tell her, but now . . . now I'm terrified. "You—you do? Okay, Brianna, I know I—"

"Greg called you, didn't he?" she says. "Your mother did say you were on the phone, after all. And well, I know you know about the . . . stuff that's happened with me and him but it's nothing, I swear, and if you want to go out with him, you should. Just be careful. I mean, he's always telling me how much he still likes me, but that's—it's talk. It's awesome that he called you."

She leans against me, her shoulder touching mine. "I can even call him tonight, if you want. Tell him he'd better be super amazing to you or else. You want me to do that?"

"You want to call him?"

"Sure. I mean, for you, of course I will." She leans over and picks up a magazine, starts flipping through it almost too casually. "Okay, who'd wear a skirt like this? It makes the model—who you know is teeny-tiny—look like Hipzilla. Look. Doesn't it?"

I pretend to look at the photo and stare at Brianna's hands holding the magazine. I know her, but I can't—I can't be right. Can I?

She likes Ryan so much that she's terrified he'll break up with her. She can't like Greg too.

"You don't have to call him," I say. "I was just watching TV. I wasn't on the phone."

"Really?"

Relief. I hear relief in her voice. I fold my hands together, stunned. "Brianna, do you—do you like Greg?"

She laughs. "You're crazy, you know that? I'm going out with Ryan, remember? I hope he tells me he loves me soon. I figure he's waiting till it's officially eight weeks, but I wish he'd just do it already. I want to hear it."

She pushes the magazine away, rolls onto her back, and looks up at my ceiling. "Ugh, I don't want to go home and deal with my mother, but if I do it, it'll be done. You're going to school tomorrow, right? No, don't answer that. You're going. You have to go."

She looks at me. "I am so sure Greg called you too, but I know that if I call him, he'll just deny calling you to tease me. But if he's all over you tomorrow, I'll know you've been keeping a secret." She singsongs the last word and then sits up and gives me a quick hug.

"Remember what I said about him though, okay?" she says, and after she's gone I realize she never really answered my question. She never said if she likes Greg or not.

Maybe she does. Maybe Greg is the one she really wants.

But I know he's not.

I know because she did tell me one thing.

She told me she hopes Ryan tells her he loves her soon.

twenty-eight

"So," Dad says in the morning. "How are you feeling?"

We're sitting at the kitchen table, both of us eating breakfast.

"Better," I say, although I'm not. I didn't want Ryan to call last night. I did want him to call. He didn't and I was glad and sad and . . . confused. I really do feel like two people sometimes.

One me wants Brianna to be okay because she's my best friend and I hate how her parents hurt her.

One me wants her to be okay so Ryan can tell her it's over.

No, I'm definitely not feeling better. Just split in two, and I don't know how to put myself back together again.

Mom calls my name as I'm heading for the front door. "Sarah, is Brianna all right?"

"I think so. I mean, as much as she can be."

"And you—are you all right?"

"I swear I'm feeling better, Mom."

"That's not—yesterday, you were on the phone, Sarah. I couldn't hear who you were talking to, but it was pretty obvious who it was."

I stare at her. She knows.

She puts a hand on my arm, her eyes full of concern. "Do you know what you're doing, Sarah?"

"No," I say, and to my surprise, she hugs me.

"Be careful," she says, and then kisses my cheek. Says, "Brianna's here."

I walk outside slowly.

As me and Brianna leave, I see Mom in the kitchen with Dad, the two of them sitting together at the kitchen table, talking. They look so happy.

"Do you think we all end up like our parents?" I ask her.

"No," Brianna says, her voice sharp, surprised, and after a moment she says, "Do I—do I act like *her*?"

Her hands are clenched tight on the steering wheel and I shake my head, say, "It was a stupid question. Just thinking about my mom and her cooking and stuff."

"You can't cook at all," Brianna says, hands relaxing a little. She grins at me. "Hey, grab my purse and use the brush in it to fix your hair because it's a little everywhere right now."

I do, thinking about what I said. Brianna isn't like her mother. Not really. She looks out for me, and okay, sometimes the stuff she says hurts, but her mother just wants Brianna to think she's nothing. Brianna keeps me from fading into that.

"I—thanks for yesterday," she says as we pull into the parking lot. "Listening to me about my dad and all that. It was—you were great, like always. Mom was . . . well, you can guess how she was."

"That bad?"

"Yeah. She was so happy. She's getting what she wants, and said he can call her whatever makes him happy as long as he understands he has to pay for me. She didn't—didn't say anything about him not wanting to see me again."

"That . . ." Even for her mother, that's bad. "I'm sorry."

"Yeah," she says, and then shakes her head. "Let's go, okay?"

"Sure," I say, and as we walk into school, I wish I could make her parents stop being such assholes. I want them to stop seeing her as a thing. I want them to be what parents are supposed to be.

"Don't," she says, as we head down the hallway.

"Don't what?"

"Worry," she says, squeezing one of my hands gently. "I'm fine, really. I can handle Mom. And it's not like Dad was ever around that much anyway."

"It still sucks."

She shrugs, then smiles at me. "I've got you." She waves at Ryan, who is standing at the end of the hall, looking at us. "And him. What more do I need?"

"Me," Greg says, coming up beside us. He slings an arm around me as he grins at Brianna, who grins back but keeps heading toward Ryan.

I stop. I can't go closer. Not to Ryan. Not now.

"So," Greg says. "What are you doing tonight?"

I look at him. He's crazy about Brianna, I know it, and I know what this is.

"I don't know what I'm doing, but I do know Brianna has plans and if you're hoping to see her—Greg, she has a boyfriend. And even if I knew where they were going, I wouldn't tell you."

"I know you won't, but she will," he says. "You'll see. I know how she is. She likes games. I do too. That's why we're perfect for each other. Tell her I said that when she asks about me."

"She won't ask," I say, but he's right.

She does ask. She comes up to me between classes and says, "What did Greg want when you two were talking before?"

I stare at her. "He said you'd ask about him and that you two are perfect for each other."

She rolls her eyes. "I bet he did."

"Why do you even care what he said?"

"I don't. I mean, it's Greg, it's not a big deal, I was just wondering, that's all. . . ." She trails off when I don't say anything, then says, "Sarah, I see you making your squinty face, and it's really not worth it. I just wanted to know what you talked about. What he said. That's it. It's like a game, you know?"

"That's exactly what he said," I say, and Brianna looks away, like something off to the side has caught her eye and she didn't hear me.

But I know she did.

twenty-nine

I see Ryan after lunch. It's noisy, the halls crowded like always, but then his eyes meet mine and when that happens the noise fades away. Everything fades away, and all I see is him.

I just see him, and it's terrifying how easily he gets to me, how he's shaped my heart.

We pass each other, and the careful second when we do lasts forever and not nearly long enough. My gaze is caught by his, he is still all I can see, and then our fingers brush against each other, no accident—I won't pretend, I can't—in a caress that lasts the blink of an eye but leaves me with the imprint of his hand against mine.

And then he says, "I have to talk to you," and touches my arm. Just skims his fingers across it, but it startles me. Moves me. Makes me realize he's moved even closer, and that I want him closer still.

"I'm talking to her tonight," he says. "I know things were bad with her dad yesterday, and that she's still upset, but I don't—I don't want to see you for a second in the hall like this. I don't want to say hi and move on. I want . . . I want us to be real. I want to be just you and me."

"You're talking to her tonight?" My head swims, my heart is pounding hard, and this is everything I've wanted, he's everything I want, but now—

Now I'm scared. I hadn't known it would be like this between us, that it would be something I can't control. That it would make me say, "Okay," and mean it.

And I do. I actually say, "Okay," and I mean it. Okay, I want him to talk to Brianna. Okay, I want it to be over for them. Okay, I want to be with him and not for a brief moment in the hall like he said.

Okay, I want us to be together. Be real.

I've been taught that love is beautiful and kind, but it isn't like that at all. It is beautiful, but it's a terrible beauty, a ruthless one, and you fall—you *fall*, and the thing is—

The thing is you want to. You don't care what's coming, you just want who your heart beats for.

"I'm pretty sure she knows I want to break up, but I want to— I've already messed up enough," Ryan says. "I wish I'd just kept talking to you that first night, I wish I hadn't been so afraid to say what I wanted to." His face is bleak.

Left unspoken is something we both know.

He'll tell her they're over, and maybe she does already know, but it will still hurt her.

He will hurt her.

I could say stop. I could say I don't want him. I could lie. I know how to do that, don't I?

I don't say anything, though. I just stand there, silent, the two of us together but not. And then the bell rings and we have to move away, both of us carried to the rest of our day.

I stumble through it as best I can, scared and excited, and then Brianna finds me after school, her hand on my arm making me jump like she's shocked me.

"What's up with you?" she says. "First Ryan totally vanishes after saying he'll see me tonight—and that was this morning—and then you weren't waiting at my car. How long have you been standing here by your locker? Don't you know we've got to go?"

I hesitate. Should I get a ride home with her? Act like everything is fine when it isn't?

"Sarah," she says, impatient, and I start to shake my head, start to say that I have something to do. I know Mom will come get me if I call.

"Okay, I was going to do this when we got to the car, but I totally can't wait anymore—look, a present!" she says, and hands me a small box, neatly wrapped and tied with a tiny blue bow.

I stare at it.

"You didn't know, right?" Brianna says. "It was so hard not to tell you this morning, but I wanted to wait until after school to give it to you."

"What—why did you do this?" I say, and my voice comes out faint, watery.

"Because, best friend, duh," Brianna says, grinning at me. "Open it!" She's happy, so damn happy, and I do, my fingers clumsy on the box.

Inside is a silver chain with a circle at the end.

"It means eternal friendship," Brianna says. "Or at least, that's what the lady at the store I got it at said it meant. I got it for your birthday but after yesterday, you totally deserve it now."

I start to cry.

"Hey," Brianna says, and wraps an arm around me, steering me outside to her car. "It's a necklace. You're just supposed to say thank you, not cry. Are you going to put it on?"

I put it on. My hands are shaking. I want to tell her everything. I want to go home and wait all this out.

This is the worst things will ever be. Today, right now, is the worst I will ever feel.

Except it's not.

thirty

Brianna doesn't take me home.

I don't notice, though. Not at first. I'm too busy running a
finger around the necklace I'm wearing and remembering
Brianna rescuing me in kindergarten. How I know she hates
cottage cheese, loves chocolate hazelnut spread, and has to
sleep with an old pillowcase that her grandmother gave her. I
know it was the only thing she managed to hide when her mom
got rid of everything her grandmother had ever given them
after she died.

I know that right after that, when her dad finally left for
good, Brianna didn't eat anything for three days, until I cried
and told her she'd die if she'd didn't (I'd just seen one of those

TV movies about eating disorders and it had terrified me) and she blinked at me slowly and said, "You'd care if I died?"

I hadn't known exactly how awful her mother made her feel until then. I hadn't realized that with her father gone, Brianna's mother turned all that's wrong with her and her life on Brianna.

I drop the necklace, letting its soft weight settle around my neck, and then realize we're turning into her driveway.

"I thought—" I say, and then break off because I feel too guilty to tell her that she should take me home. That I want to go home.

"I know, I usually take you home and we hang out there, but—okay," she says. "Last night, after I got home and Mom was . . . well, Mom . . . I stayed up late because I couldn't sleep and made brownies."

"You made brownies?"

"I know," she says. "Surprised me too, but after I wrapped your necklace I was thinking about how great you've been this year—not that you aren't always great, but sometimes you're a little judgy. Anyway, lately you've been totally supportive, so I wanted to thank you."

"I—I need some air or something," I say, and open the car door. I want to throw up, I want that big dramatic moment like you see and read about, I want to actually be so sick of myself and what I've done that my body revolts against me, but instead I just stare at the ground, my stomach churning.

And then Brianna is out of the car and kneeling in front of me, peering up at me and nudging the necklace so it swings back and forth, smiling. "Come on, let's go eat brownies."

"I can't," I say, looking at the necklace, and she takes my arm and says, "You can do whatever you want. Free will means making your own choices, right? I'm pretty sure of that one. We just talked about it in my stupid philosophy class. Worst elective ever."

"Yeah," I say, and the word is so bitter in my mouth. I've made my choices, and I made them all knowing everything.

I know what I should do. I know this is where I *have* to tell her everything.

But I don't, and the worst part is, I know I won't.

I've had chances—so many chances—and I've kept silent.

Why? Because I know Ryan, and I know that when he talks to her tonight, when he ends it with her, he won't say it's because of me. I know the part I've played will be kept silent.

I want me and Ryan to get together and Brianna to never know that one kiss turned out to be so right that I didn't want to let it go. I don't want Brianna to be mad at me, and if she knows what's happened, what I've done, she will be. I want Ryan, but I want to keep my best friend too, and there's a way to do that because Brianna will never guess he looked at me when he was with her, not ever.

"See, brownies!" she says when we walk into the kitchen and points at a small plate of them on the counter. She picks it up, takes off the plastic wrap, and sits down at the kitchen table.

I don't hesitate. I sit down too and pick up a brownie, heavy with chocolate chunks. Chocolate doesn't cure everything, although Mom has an apron that says so, but it does taste good, and if I'm eating, I don't have to think about talking. I don't have to tell myself I will in a minute, or that I just need to find a way to start.

I don't have to hate myself for lying.

"So, I'm a pretty good cook, right?" Brianna says as I start on my second brownie. She pulls a chocolate chunk out of hers and pops it in her mouth. "I think hanging out around your mom is rubbing off on me."

She grins. "Or maybe I just used a mix and put chocolate pieces in it. Don't tell your mom, okay? I know how she feels about mixes." She lowers her voice, adds, "And don't tell my mom either. I took the chocolate from her stash in the freezer."

"You did what?" I say, startled, because Brianna is always very careful about not messing with her mother's stuff.

"She's getting everything she ever wanted from Dad. She can spare a chocolate bar or two. Or three," Brianna says, still grinning, but it's tighter now. Sadder.

"You know we have to be friends until we're both senile now, right?" she says. "I mean, brownies *and* a necklace. You can't top that, can you?" She's trying to sound like she's kidding, but that's the thing about being Brianna's best friend. I know when she really means something. I know when she is hurting.

I know when she needs me to make her feel better.

"It's untoppable," I say. "Or it is until you're famous and I can tell people I know you, the superstar actress."

"You can be my assistant," she says. "Answer my fan mail, help me with my lines."

"When do you find out if you got the lead in the play?"

"Soon," she says. "It's some Shakespeare thing, but we're doing a modern adaptation of it—you heard us talking about it that night you came over with my clothes."

I look at my brownie as she keeps talking.

"Knowing Mrs. Leslie, that means all the girls will be in guys' roles and the guys will be playing girls. Which isn't very modern, really, since it used to be nothing but guys in all the plays. But whatever. I just have to get through tryouts."

"You'll be great."

"You think?"

I nod. Brianna is happiest when she's acting. When she can be someone else, step into a world that isn't this one, a world that doesn't have her parents and how they make her feel in it.

"Okay, two more bites and then I'm done," she says. "Should I wear my blue shirt tonight? Ryan likes it, but I think I look better in the pink one, the one with the lace. Not that Ryan won't stare at my chest anyway, because he always does, but—"

"Hey, what would happen if some guy started liking you but ended up liking me instead?" I say, interrupting, and the sugar has made me stupid or maybe it's what she's said about Ryan looking at her. Or maybe I'm saying what I should, maybe I'm finally starting a conversation I know we need to have.

I look at her, and wait for her reply.

"I thought you said you didn't like Greg," she says.

"I—that's not what I said. I said if a guy liked you and decided he liked me, what would you think?"

"Sarah," Brianna says, leaning over and putting her arms around me. "You know I love you. You're adorable, and I'm convinced there's a freshman out there who's as cute as you are just waiting for you. But Greg won't ever really like you because the guys who like me don't—you and I are just really—well, we're different looking, you know? You look like a little sister kind of girl. Sweet and comfortable."

"And you're not?" I say, pulling away, and my hands are shaking now, not from sadness but anger, because I hear what she's saying. I know *exactly* what she means. I don't make guys want. And she does.

"I don't think anyone's ever called me sweet," she says, and takes another bite of brownie. "I like to keep guys on their toes. Make them work. It's more fun that way."

"For you? Or them?"

"Okay, what's up with the pissy voice?" she says. "I thought you just said this wasn't about Greg."

"Well, girls, I see some people at least get to relax," Brianna's mother says from behind us, and I watch Brianna's face freeze, then fall. I watch her mother glance very pointedly at the brownies and see Brianna flush, ashamed when she doesn't need to be.

"I actually ate most of the brownies," I say, and Brianna's mother glances at me briefly and says, "Hello, Sarah," coolly before turning back to Brianna.

"Well, you might as well finish it," she says, pointing to the brownie Brianna is hastily putting down, and then turns, peering at something over the sink. I brace myself for another outburst until I realize she's caught sight of herself in the window and is smoothing her hair, making sure every strand is in place.

"Are you here tonight?" she says, turning back to Brianna and opening her purse. "I'm having a friend come pick me up, and then we're going for a drink. Peter's younger than I am, but says he finds it impossible to believe."

She laughs lightly and pulls out a tube of lipstick, frowns at it, and then tosses it back in. "I need some new makeup. I'll bring you home something too, I think. That last set of acne products I got you didn't work so well, did it?"

Brianna gets about one pimple every six months and it's always high up on her forehead, so high that she can cover it with her hair.

"Thanks, and no, I'm not here. I'm going out," Brianna mutters, and her mother comes over to the table, touches the top of her head, and says, "I'm off to change. Do something with your hair if you really are going out, sweetie. It would be so much prettier if you brushed it once in a while."

Brianna stuffs the last of the brownie she was eating into her mouth, and her mother sighs and leaves the kitchen.

I move toward her, shifting in my chair, but she shakes her head, gets up, and goes out onto the deck. I wait a few seconds because I know she needs them and then follow her.

"And that's the parent who wants me," she says as I walk up to her. She's staring out into her backyard, no sadness on her face. No anger. No expression except resignation. Weariness.

"I try, you know? I do. But my dad doesn't even want to see me and my mom thinks I'm hopeless. And what if—what are you if the people who are supposed to love you can leave you like you're nothing?"

"Brianna—"

"I'm sick of it," she says. "I don't need to—I don't need to feel like this again, not ever. Why do you think I always go out with guys who are pathetic over me? I know they won't leave me, Sarah. But I want . . . just once, I want to make someone who could turn away from me decide they want to stay where they are. I want them to stay with me. I want that to happen with Ryan and it—it will. I'm going to make it happen."

"You—wait. You want Ryan because you want to make him stay with you?"

"It's not like you make it sound," she says, shaking her head. "You don't get it, Sarah. You don't know what it's like to be in love. Love is . . . you get confused and you do stuff you don't mean to do and you just—you hate yourself and some-times you don't even want to love the person you do because it would be so much easier if you didn't. But you just—you just do."

I want to tell her she's crazy and wrong, but she isn't. I know she isn't, because that's how I feel, the things she's done are things I've done and she—

She loves Ryan.

She really loves him.

I feel sick. "I—have you—have you told him?"

She sighs. "No, because it's—how can you say it when you're wondering why the guy doesn't love you back? It's hard to even think about it. But I . . . I can do this. I will do this. I can get what I want. I just . . . can you just pretend you understand and stay with me for a little while?"

thirty-one

I don't want her to love him.

It was one thing to want Ryan when I didn't know that she feels the same way I do. That he fills her heart like he fills mine.

She loves him, and her wanting to be with him isn't about her knowing that he doesn't like her the way she wants him to. It's that she likes him more than he likes her. It's that she sees it and doesn't know what to do about it.

She's scared. She doesn't want to be left.

She wants to be loved, and so I stay with her. I watch her try on outfits, I watch out for Brianna's mother, who likes to dart in and offer advice, poisonous words that make Brianna's shoulders sag even when she's feeling unstoppable. And she isn't feeling that way tonight.

"You look great," I tell Brianna after her mother slithers in and makes her smile tremble, and her mother says, "Brianna, you certainly do have a loyal friend. What a lucky girl you are!"

Her voice is sugar-filled fakery, and when she goes, Brianna grins at me. "Okay, now I'm totally giving you another brownie to eat when I drive you home. I may even put a candle in it to celebrate your awesomeness. And I'm going to tell Ryan about it too, so he knows how awesome you are."

Ryan. Tonight. She loves him.

And he's going to break up with her.

"I—"

"Don't tell me I can't praise you," she says. "Now just let me finish my makeup and we'll go."

The doorbell rings then, and Brianna's mother yells, "Brianna, get that, and tell Peter I'll be right down. And if he asks if we're sisters, say yes!"

I stand up and Brianna glances at me in the mirror, panic and shame flashing in her eyes.

"Like I'd let you do that," I say. "Please."

"You're a star," Brianna says, and I nod, then head downstairs. I don't want to think about tonight.

It is all I can think about. At least I get to do this.

I open the front door with a flourish, ready to puncture Brianna's mother a little, and then stop, mouth open, door handle digging into my hand because I'm gripping it so hard.

"Sarah?" Ryan says.

thirty-two

We stare at each other for a moment, silent, and
then Ryan steps inside hesitantly, still looking at me.

I should move back, I'm too close to the door, I am so close I
could reach out and touch him, tug on his shirt and pull him close,
pull him to me, and he is looking at my mouth, I can see it, I can
feel it, and everything inside me is screaming his name, screaming
for him.

And then Brianna comes downstairs.

I don't see her—I hear her—and she clears her throat, says,
"Hey there, you're early," and I turn to her, say, "It's not Peter," stupidly, blindly, and watch her gaze flicker over me. She looks pretty
and happy.

"I know, I recognize my own boyfriend." She laughs, but it

doesn't reach her eyes and she is looking at me strangely.

At least, I think she is. I don't know, I can't tell, guilt and panic are making a mess of my insides. Of me.

"Yeah, I—here he is," I say, still talking. Why am I still talking?

Ryan says, "Hey," to Brianna, and I know the necklace should be burning white-hot against my neck but things like that only happen in fairy tales and instead I just finger it, Brianna's gaze on me but then turning away, turning to Ryan.

"So, I forgive you for vanishing during school after being all 'we have to talk,'" she says, walking to him, and I have seen her walk like this so many times, perfect-looking, somehow seeming to almost glide across the floor.

Face turned up ever so slightly. Ready for a kiss.

"Actually, I tried to find you," Ryan says. "But you weren't any-where I looked and I—"

"You found me now," Brianna says, and she's going to kiss him, she's moving in closer and closer.

"I'll—I'll go call my parents and have one of them come get me," I say, and Brianna says, "Just take my car. I'll have Ryan drop me off at your house later. Much later."

I hear her mother moving around upstairs, watch Brianna flash a wicked smile at Ryan and motion for them to go, her hand on his arm, and she gets to do that, of course she does.

Her smile, so full of promise, of *them*, is all I can see as I start to turn away, as I watch her close that last bit of distance between them.

I hear the soft sounds of a kiss, of their voices whispering, and how can I want him to break up with her and yet be so scared of how upset she'll be? How can I be so screwed up?

"Wait," Brianna says. "Bowling? Your big plan for tonight is bowling? Don't you see my shirt?"

"I thought . . ." Ryan clears his throat. "I like bowling."

Brianna mutters, "You would."

Wait, this is love? This is Brianna in love?

I don't get it. But I do know I have got to get out of here.

There's just one thing. I need Brianna's keys, and they are right where she left them, with her purse on the weird little bench by the front door.

They are right where she and Ryan are, and as I decide I'll sneak out, wait for them to go, and then just come back in and get them somehow, she says, "Hey, Sarah."

I turn and look at her.

"I know you heard all that just now," she says. "And if I have to go bowling, I need people around me to at least make sure there's some fun. So you're coming." She points to the kitchen. "Go call your parents. Ryan, my mom's here, so you'd better wait in your car. I'm going to get shoes that won't be wasted sitting in a cubby in the oh-so-lovely bowling alley."

"Oh," Ryan says, and glances at me again quickly, so quickly, before he goes back outside, making my heart, my stupid, traitorous heart, pound in spite of everything.

When he leaves, Brianna doesn't go up to her room, but heads for her mother's office.

"What are you doing?" I say, but she doesn't answer.

I sigh and call home.

thirty-three

As I'm calling my parents, I don't know what to do. Brianna wants me there, with them, tonight.

And Ryan's going to break up with her. How can I see that? Especially now that I know she loves him. I—

There aren't even words for this.

I rest my head against the wall as my parents' phone rings. Once, twice, and I press myself into the wall, hard, like I can somehow push myself inside it.

"Hey," I say, voice shaking, when Dad answers the phone. "I'm going out with Brianna and Ryan, okay?"

"What?" Dad says, distracted sounding.

"I'm going out," I say again. "And don't worry about me getting home, I have a ride."

"Dad?" I say after a moment, after he hasn't said anything, and he's old, I know, but he's not that old, not really, not ancient grandfather old, and if he was sick Mom wouldn't let him answer the phone. Although she usually answers it because she's always waiting for a call from a contesting friend or about a cook-off.

A cook-off. Like the Fabulous Family Cook-Off.

"Dad," I say again. "What happened? What's going on?"

"Your mother isn't—she won't be getting a call," he says.

"What? How does she know that? They were supposed to call all weekend."

"Your mother's friend Jillian, the one who won the Cozy Cakes Contest, got a call and then called your mother," Dad says. "Apparently Fabulous Family decided to call all the finalists today to keep people from having to wait by the phone all weekend."

"Cutting costs," I hear Mom say in the background, and her voice is very high, like it gets when she's really upset. The last time I heard her sound like this was when a judge came up to her after the Clucky Pluck Chicken cook-off and told her she'd have placed if her dish hadn't gotten cold before they'd been able to try it. "It's cheaper to call everyone today and not have people work all weekend. And nicer too, so nice for the finalists to find out now instead of waiting . . ."

I hear a muffled noise, a sob, and Dad says, "Honey, don't—" and then, "Sarah, I'm taking your mother out to dinner and then to The Adams. We'll be back in the morning."

Dad has taken Mom to The Adams, which is a super fancy and expensive hotel about an hour away, exactly twice. Once on their fifteenth wedding anniversary, and then again last year after the doctor told him his arthritis was only going to get worse and Mom was so sad she stopped cooking for a while.

"Can I talk to her?" I say, and there's more silence, then low murmuring, and then Mom is on the phone, her voice quiet and teary.

"Sarah, I'm all right. Your father is just being nice. I really don't need—" She breaks off, makes that horrible sound people do when they're trying not to cry, a sob that sort of rattles in the throat. "I don't need to be in this cook-off or any other. It's just something I do for fun, that's all, but I let myself think that I . . ."

She makes the noise again.

"Mom, I'm so sorry," I say. "Do you want me to come home?"

"No," she says. "You don't need to see your mother crying over not getting into a cook-off. I'm embarrassed I'm doing it, but I—" Her voice drops to a sad whisper. "I really wanted it to happen. I thought it would. I thought I did everything right."

"You did. You totally did, and if they can't see how great you are, then they suck."

"You shouldn't say things like that," Mom says, but her voice is auto-pilot Mom, not serious, and I say, "Even if they're true?" and she sighs.

"I just wish I knew what I did wrong. I was so sure that I'd be going. I shouldn't have—it was stupid to think I'd be picked."

"No, it wasn't," I say, and hear Dad, in the background, say the same thing too.

"All right," Mom says, and her voice isn't quite as sad sounding now. "Not stupid, then. Just a reminder that you don't always get everything you want."

I blink once, hard, as a chill shudders up my spine because she's right and I know it. I know it, and that scares me.

I know I want too much.

What will happen because of that?

"Are you sure you don't want me to come home?" I say, clearing my throat, and Mom says, "No, but your father and I will be coming home after dinner at The Adams, so—"

"No, we won't," Dad says, getting on the phone again. "Your mother needs to relax and that's what she's going to do. Call us if you need anything, though, and we'll be home early tomorrow afternoon."

I hang up just as Brianna comes back into the kitchen.

"Ready?" she says, and I nod.

I wait for her to ask what my parents said, or how they are. She usually wants to know that.

"Great, let's just go already then," she says, and doesn't ask about my parents at all.

"Are you okay?" I say, and then hear her mother coming downstairs. I smell her perfume, which is all sweet flowers, lovely and calming, but whenever I get a whiff of it I just want to run.

Brianna doesn't say anything, just takes my hand and rushes us both outside. I squeeze her fingers once, gently, to let her know that I'm here, and she doesn't squeeze back, just lets go and says, "You drive, okay?" holding her keys out toward me.

"You—you want to go with me? What about Ryan?"

"He'll follow," she says, and gets in the car.

And so we drive off, me and her together, with Ryan behind us.

Brianna doesn't say a word on the way to the bowling alley and I—well, for once I don't feel split in two. I am one person right now and that person is very confused.

And very scared.

thirty-four

At the bowling alley, Brianna is a weird mix of bored and hyper, talking whenever Ryan starts to say something and then sighing off into space when he's silent, shooting me glances that say, "Can you believe this?"

I smile back tentatively, and she says, "Okay, refreshment run," and grabs my hand, tows us toward the snack bar.

"I can't believe he brought me here," she says after we get sodas. "Almost two months and this is it? I know we had our first sort of date here, but still. I don't even think he knows how upset I am and—oh, of course. I should have known this would happen."

I follow her gaze, see that Greg and a bunch of other people from school have come in. They all head straight for us.

"Bowling, huh?" Greg says to Brianna. "What are the odds?"

"Stalker," she says, but she's grinning, and I realize what she was doing when I called my parents.

She called Greg. She told him to come meet her. And I just go numb.

I follow them blindly and look at her, at my best friend, sitting down next to Greg, pushing him away when he rubs her knee, but gently, teasingly, and then I get why all this is happening.

Brianna wants Ryan to be exactly where she wants him to be and no place else. She wants him with her, and she wants him to love her, just like she said.

But she doesn't love him.

She doesn't love him at all.

She doesn't trust love—she runs from it, she leaves it behind. All the guys who have really cared for her have been left behind and I know that. I've seen it. Brianna wants the people who are supposed to love her to look at her with their hearts, and her parents look at her and think only of themselves. It's what she knows, and anything else—anything that she knows, deep down, could be real—falls into a category she doesn't like.

That she's terrified of.

But then where does that leave me? The sister she says she's never had but that I am, the best friend who has always been by her side.

She tells me she loves me.

Does she?

"Brianna?" I say.

"What?" she says, distracted-sounding.

"Can we talk for a second?"

"Sure," Brianna says, laughing as Greg winks at her, and then gets up and loops her arm through mine, drawing me off a little to the side. "What's up?"

"You—you don't—you and Ryan—"

"Me and Ryan what?" she says. "I know we're not talking now, but I need to give him a little space. He's like that."

"No," I say. "That's not it, that's not why. You don't—Brianna, you don't love him."

"Of course I do," she says, but her smile wavers a bit.

"Not everyone is going to leave you," I say. "You know that, right? I mean, your parents—"

"What are you talking about?" she says, cutting me off, her voice sharp. "No one leaves me. I always get bored and find someone better. That's what happens."

"I know," I say softly. "I just—you do know I'm never going to leave you. Don't you?"

She stares at me, her face still, expressionless, and then she smiles, not her real smile, but her Brianna smile, the one she shows the world when it gets to her, the one that says she's fine, everything is fine. The one that means nothing.

"Of course I know that. You need me. I mean, who would you be without me?" She flicks her hair back, says, "There's a comb in my bag. Use it, okay? Your hair will look way better if you do."

And then she's gone, heading back to everyone else. Ryan says her name as she passes him, says, "Hey, Brianna, can we talk?" and her eyes go wide for a moment before she grins her Brianna grin and walks back to Greg, sitting back down beside him.

I sit down and yank off my shoes, fighting back tears, and then I go to the rental counter and turn them in.

I'm going. Brianna doesn't need me, she said I need her, she doesn't even see me as a person. I am just a thing that—

I am just a thing to her.

Has it always been this way?

No. I can't believe that. I know—I know she has turned to me. Talked to me. I touch the necklace, remember her face when she gave it to me.

I take a deep breath and walk over to her.

"You're leaving, I guess," she says, looking bored and sounding annoyed, holding out a hand for her car keys. When I pass them to her, I see what I've done.

I've told her I see her—really see her—and she doesn't like it. She doesn't like it at all. She needs me to be the Sarah she knows, the one who has always been her happy shadow.

She needs me to need her.

"I am," I say, because I can't do this—be this person, be the Sarah she wants—right now. I don't even want to be around her.

I start to head outside, taking off the necklace and sliding it into my pocket. I can't wear it right now, and as for getting home, I'll just catch a ride with someone when they leave.

I look back as I reach the door, and everyone is clustered around Brianna. Even the old people who are there to bowl are aware of her, cast glances at her out of the corners of their eyes.

I see Ryan walk up to her.

I stop, hear someone say, "Are you leaving or what?" and then

I am shaking my head and turning, walking slowly back into the bowling alley and watching Brianna get up, exasperation on her face as she stares at Ryan.

"Look," she says. "I thought bowling would suck, but it's not so bad and yet you're just sitting around looking all whatever, and you know what? I don't feel like dealing with it. With you."

"I really need to talk to you, okay?" Ryan says, and Brianna laughs, hair rippling down her back.

"You need, you need, I get it, it's you you you. What is it with guys?" She looks at everyone gathered around, everyone acting as if they aren't hanging on every word even though they are. Everyone is listening, she's got her voice raised now and it's carrying, this is Brianna 101, this is Brianna when—

"I'm done," she says, and this is Brianna when she leaves. "You and me—it's not working. I need some time to think, and I can't do it with you trying to 'talk' to me every five seconds. I just—I can't deal with you now, okay? I don't want to see you now. So go."

"Go? You mean we're—"

"Are you going to repeat everything I say? Do you not get what 'go' means?" Brianna says, and why is she dumping him now? She told me she loves him, she looked at me and said she did.

But she also said she doesn't want to be left anymore, and Ryan was right. On some level, she knew what was coming.

So she's left him.

She's ended it, and I head outside. I stand in the parking lot, my heart beating so hard I feel strange, light-headed, like I've drifted into another world. Brianna said she was going to stay with

Ryan, that she wanted to keep him with her. She sounded so sure and I never thought—

I never thought she'd let him go.

"Sarah?"

But she did, she did, and he is here now, he is in the parking lot, and I turn toward him.

"Hey," he says. "What are you doing out here?"

I swallow. "Waiting for a ride."

"Oh. Are . . . how long are you going to have to wait?"

"I don't know."

"Can I . . . can I give you a ride home?"

She's left him. She's told him she doesn't want to see him. He's free now.

We're both free.

I nod, and he smiles.

thirty-five

Being with Ryan is like—it's like opening a door
to a room that has always been there, waiting.

It's easy, the kind of easy that feels right. Perfect.

When we get to my house, he parks in the garage and listens
when I tell him about my parents, about Mom's failed attempt to
enter the Fabulous Family Cook-Off. He knew she'd been trying
to get there, of course, he's been on the fringes of my life for a
while now.

He smiles when I say that to him.

"Years," he says. "I've wanted to be here, really here, like this,
with you, since eighth grade."

"Me too," I say, naked words, honest words. They are real.

We are real.

We kiss then, in the garage, not in romantic splendor of moonlight or candlelight or anything like that. We don't kiss in the glow of a party, where everyone can—and will—see. We kiss in private, there in the dark in his car. We kiss and I know I will never ever have another kiss like it, that there will never be another moment like this one, where I feel so alive, so new, so free.

So happy.

I know Brianna just broke up with him, I know this is all so fast, and maybe I should slow down and not get caught up in this. In Ryan and me.

But I want to be caught.

"Do you want to come in?" I say, and I know I should be playing it safe, that I should be thinking about everything that's happened tonight. Letting him have time to think about it.

I don't need time, though. Not to figure out how I feel. And I know he doesn't either.

He answers me with another kiss, and we are both breathing heavily when we separate, our smiles shining at each other.

His fingers catch mine, lace through them, as we walk inside, and we don't talk. I don't feel like I have to, I don't feel like this silence needs to be filled. I'm not nervous, I'm not overwhelmed by having him here. By being with him.

I have pictured him here, like this, a hundred, no, a million times since I realized I liked him back in eighth grade, and never in sugar-coated dreams of gentle conversation.

No, I always wanted this, what I'm doing now, heading

upstairs with him, feeling his hand, bigger and warmer than mine, worn rough in spots from the pictures he's drawn and the work that shaped him over the summer, turned him from the skinny guy I longed for into the lanky, muscled one I long for too.

In my room he looks around, fingers still wrapped around mine, seeing everything that makes me who I am, the sneakers spilling out of my closet, the little sketches I've done of shoes I want to make tacked on my wall, and the laundry on the floor Mom always nags me to pick up.

I don't worry about any of this. I know I don't have to explain why I like what I do, who I am. I don't have to apologize for not being perfect. All I have to do is be here, be me—and I am. So when he turns to me, smiling and motioning at my sketches, I step toward him, step into his arms.

"I've always liked your shoes," he says. "I've always liked you," and then we are hugging, and I've been hugged plenty but not like this, never like this, because Ryan's arms are around me, he's smiling down at me.

He's holding me, and then his mouth meets mine again.

We end up on my bed, wrapped around each other, and it's enough, it's more than enough. There is no pressure, no rushing, nothing Ryan and I have to do.

We just are. That's it. That's all we have to be.

Around two in the morning his stomach rumbles and I grin at him, our legs twined together. I am still in my clothes and he is still in his but I am the most naked I have ever been, we have spent hours lying together just watching each other, touching and kissing and talking and I am filled with joy, incandescent.

This is what happiness is, past the rubbish of its overuse as a word, past the cracked gloss of the letters that mean nothing when strung together. They mean something now, and I know what it's like when you and someone else are right together. How simple it is, and how amazing.

"Hungry?" I say, and we walk downstairs, my hand clasped in his. We stand in the kitchen making sandwiches together, moving as if we are one, him standing behind me as I pull out the bread, my arms wrapped around him as he spreads peanut butter in a thick layer and then tops it with sliced apple.

I shake my head when he offers me half and he says, "You still won't eat apples? Really?" and he knows that, remembers that from years ago when, for a time, we faced an apple a day on our middle school lunch trays and I always gave mine away or tossed it in the trash.

He cares, he knows me, and it makes my insides hum, glow with something so much stronger than desire, which—I admit—I feel plenty of too.

We eat our sandwiches in the light of the moon spilling into the kitchen, plain peanut butter for me and apples and peanut butter for him, and then we are kissing again, kissing like no one else in the world has ever discovered it, and maybe they haven't, because I don't think anyone knows the sweetness, the rightness, of watching Ryan put his plate in the sink, of him turning to me.

Of his slow smile and the way he reaches for me as if he's exactly where he should be, where he wants to be. Of the impatient waiting for his mouth to meet mine and the way both of us pause, mouths a breath apart, on fire with waiting and then burning up, reduced to ash by the mere touch of our mouths, kissing until I don't know where he ends and I begin and it doesn't matter because I don't care. I just want this to go on forever.

We finally fall asleep as the sun starts to rise, his hand stroking my hair as pink pierces the sky and pales the stars.

"I love you," he whispers as my eyes are fluttering closed, and when I open them, happy, so happy, I see my smile shining in his.

"I didn't want to tell you too soon, so I waited until you were asleep," he says, grinning, and then we are both laughing, bathed in the slow rising light of the morning sun. I sit up and touch his shoulders, feeling his skin under my hands and see him looking up at me, his hands touching my skin with slow, hot movements, little circles up and down my sides that make me arch toward him.

"I love you too," I say, and the words float out of me like wings, soar into the air, and later, when he arches above me and says, "We have time," a tiny question in his voice, not worry but wonder, I nod.

I say, "So much time," and sleep won't come now, not with my blood singing in me, and that is the best part of all. That we do have time. That what we have will be. That we are.

But of course I do fall asleep.

I wake up, see the clock says ten and look at him, at his dark hair falling across his forehead, at the way the sunlight shines on his skin, and remember touching it.

I move closer, pressing my skin to his, my only thought touching him again, having him touch me, and he opens his eyes slowly, blinking.

"Sleepy," I say, and worry, for a moment, about my breath, my narrow body, my unbrushed hair, and then it is gone, wiped away by his smile, by how he breathes, "Sarah," and looks at me as if I'm the sun, and the stars. As if I'm everything.

I ask him about his parents because I have just remembered mine and his eyes go wide. He sits up, reaches for my phone, and calls them. I listen as he says he's fine, that he's sorry he didn't call, as his hand gently squeezes mine. I can hear his father's voice, raised, on the other end of the line, but I can't make out the words.

"I'm really sorry I didn't call, okay? I didn't want to wake you and Mom up. But yes, I'm alive. And yes, I'm with a friend." Sideways smile at me, and my breath catches. "Oh, don't—all right, fine. I'll do it."

He sighs, hanging up the phone, and says, "Penance. I have to make lunch for everyone today."

"You can cook?"

"You saw me last night," he says, and I grin at him and he grins back and then we are sliding together, his mouth on my throat, and I pull him closer, whisper his name, and this is better than the best, it is beyond it, beyond everything.

And then my door opens. Ryan and I move as one, diving for the sheets, for the blanket, pulling them up around ourselves as we sit up, and what will I say to my parents? They are understanding but not this understanding. How do I go from never talking about any guys to having one in the house, in my room, in my bed?

"What the fuck?"

It isn't my parents.

It's Brianna.

thirty-six

"What the fuck?" she says again, her voice angry, and Ryan's hand reaches for mine under the covers, holds it.

Brianna sees that and her gaze narrows, growing colder by the second. She looks at him, then me, and then walks into my room, slamming the door behind her, and the bright sun doesn't feel so perfect now, nothing feels perfect now, I see the shock and anger on her face, I see the hurt, and I say, "Brianna—"

She slaps me.

"You bitch," she says, and I'm not sure what hurts worse, her hand or the hatred in her voice, undiluted venom I've only heard aimed at other people and not at me, never at me. "I turn around for two seconds and you decide to fuck my boyfriend?"

"Brianna, no, we didn't—"

"You didn't?" she says, and then laughs, but it's a hollow sound, a mocking sound. "Of course not. Only you, Sarah, could get a guy to come back here with you and then have nothing happen. You are so clueless, so stupid—"

"Hey," Ryan says, his voice hard. "Stop it."

"What?" Brianna says, and swings her gaze to him, eyes narrowed, so narrowed.

"Stop it," Ryan says again, and his voice is a little softer now. "Brianna, I want to be here. I want Sarah. And we broke up, remember?"

"Broke up? When did we break up?" Brianna says. "Oh, wait, I get it. I tell you I need space and you freak out and turn to my friend—who clearly isn't my friend—and decide to try and get back at me. This is . . . well, this is a first. I can't believe I thought you were a nice guy, Ryan. I can't believe I thought you were special."

"We did break up, but this—Sarah and I—it isn't about you," Ryan says. "I like Sarah. I—Brianna, all the things you said last night were true. We aren't—we don't work. I'm not happy with you, and I don't think you were ever happy with me."

"I wasn't happy with you?" Brianna says. "Almost eight weeks, Ryan. Almost eight weeks and then you go and—" She glares at me. "Is this my anniversary present? You could have at least picked someone decent. Someone I'd believe you want and not who you just used to make yourself feel better."

I feel myself shrink, feel terrible and small and worthless. Brianna thinks that I'm nothing, that no one would ever turn to me, and she has known me forever, she knows me like no one else does.

And then I look at her. I see her staring at me, her mouth twisted, tears in her eyes, and I remember what she said to me last night. *You need me.*

"I should have told you some things before," I say slowly, carefully. "I—Brianna, Ryan and I—we—"

"There isn't a Ryan and you," she says, her voice rising again. "There's me and Ryan and then there's you. There's no you and Ryan, there's just him being an ass and you being pathetic, and what kind of friend are you, Sarah? What kind of fucking friend are you?"

"Brianna," Ryan says, and she looks at him, then shakes her head and says, "You don't even want to know what I want to do to you right now. You're worse than dirt, you're—you will have to grovel so hard before I even think about ever taking you back."

"I'm where I want to be," Ryan says. "I should have said something before and I'm sorry I didn't. I wish I had, but Sarah and I—"

"Sarah and I?" Brianna says. "Sarah and I? Like you two are actually something?"

"Yes," Ryan says, and Brianna's eyes fill with tears again. Her mouth starts to quiver and I tuck the sheet around me tighter, say, "Brianna—" desperate to have her listen, to not have this all fall apart. "You said it was over, I heard you say it, and I thought—"

"I know what you thought," she says. "You've been planning this, haven't you?"

I feel my skin heat, feel a blush wash over me because I have wanted this, have hoped for it, for Ryan, and she hisses out a breath and says, "Whore," her voice deadly cold.

"Brianna," Ryan says. "Don't talk about Sarah—"

"I'm not talking to you," she says, glancing at him, and then stares at me, her eyes cold.

"I don't know you," she says, her voice flat, empty. "You and I, our so-called friendship—it's done. And when it all falls apart for you, when Ryan wants me back—and he will because you aren't me, you'll never be me—I won't be there. You're nothing to me, and you'll be nothing to him too."

"That's not going to happen," Ryan says, his voice not so soft now. It's hard, angry, and I know he feels me shaking against him. Brianna smile-sneers and moves closer, moves toward us, raises her hand again, raises it toward him, and then backs off, shaking.

"You aren't worth it, Ryan," she says. "Neither of you is worth it."

And then she leaves.

I get out of bed, sheet trailing around me, and glimpse the necklace she gave me lying on the floor, peeking out of my pocket. Last night I took it off and never really once thought of her after that.

After I left with Ryan.

Brianna may not have been the friend I thought she was, but I haven't been much of one either.

I've been worse.

I race into the hall, call her name. She stops at the bottom of the stairs, but doesn't look back.

I hear her car go, wheels screeching as she pulls away, and then I sit on the stairs and cry.

Ryan comes out and sits next to me, puts his arms around me.

He doesn't say everything will be fine. He just holds me, and when I'm done crying, when I pull back a little and look at him, he cups my chin in his hand.

"I love you," he says. "And I'm sorry about what just happened. If I'd known—" He breaks off. "I can't lie to you," he says after a moment, his voice very quiet. "I wouldn't change what's happened with you and me."

I lean against his shoulder. "I know," I whisper, and the thing is, I do. I believe in him, in us. I feel the truth of what we are even now.

But Brianna—for all that she's done, all that she's said—and for what I've done as well—I can't believe our friendship is over. I can't believe I'm truly nothing to her now. I know I messed up in a way that redefines the word "mess," but we have been friends for so long. She has been my whole world for so long.

I know everything will work out. It has to, because I can't imagine my life without Brianna in it.

thirty-seven

Brianna doesn't forgive me. She won't even speak
to me. I try calling her but she won't answer the phone, and if her
mother does, she'll call for Brianna, who never comes. Sometimes
I hear Brianna's mother starting to yell at her, asking her if she
thinks she's the only person in the world before the connection is
cut and silence falls.

Brianna would rather hear her mother than me.

My parents know what's happened, of course, or at least have
guessed most of it. How could they not? Brianna doesn't come over
anymore and Ryan—well, I don't hide him. I don't want to.

"Do you miss her?" Mom says to me one night after Ryan has
left—he's drawing another series of pictures of hands, and he's

fascinated by Dad's—and I nod. She's cooking again, but not as intensely as before. She still talks about cook-offs, but not as much, and is only going to enter three next year instead of as many as she can.

"Sometimes . . . sometimes you have to let people go," she says. "Brianna loves you, Sarah, but I don't think she was always a good friend to you."

"I wasn't exactly a good friend to her either," I say, and Mom puts an arm around me.

"Maybe not, but I think you would have forgiven her anything." She kisses my cheek. "So, you and Ryan—"

"Mom!"

"I was just going to say you seem happy," she says, and I hear Dad chuckling in the other room. His hip isn't better—it won't ever be better—but it isn't worse. At least, not yet.

In school, Brianna looks right through me, doesn't turn away if I walk up to her but just stares at me as if I'm nothing, as if I'm not there.

I'm sure there will be a million people waiting to be with Brianna, to side with her, to be where I was, to be her best friend, but it doesn't happen. No one seems to really hate me or Ryan for being together, although I notice some girls hold their boyfriends' hands a little more tightly when I walk by them. Most of them are nice, though, and I find myself talking to people I haven't spoken to beyond a quick "Hi" or "Did you hear what the homework is?" before because I always had Brianna. I find myself doing things like going shopping and to the movies and laughing about school and it's nice, but it's not—it's not like it was with Brianna, and I miss her so much.

I see Brianna with other people, but they float in and out, don't stay by her side. Sometimes they come up to me and say things like, "How did you ever put up with her?" or "Okay, can I ask you something? Does she always say stuff that she thinks is being nice or helpful but totally isn't?"

"She doesn't mean it like how it sounds," I always say. "She just wants—she's a good friend," and they look at me blankly, like I am a puzzle they don't understand. Sometimes they just say, "That's not what she says about you." Those are the ones who float away fastest.

She gets the lead in the school play, and I'm not there when she finds out. I don't get to hear how she's going to play Romeo as a girl, I don't get to hear how she feels about Henry being her Juliet. I can picture it, but it's not the same. I'm not there.

I don't hear about the practices, about how she's learning her lines. I don't hear about opening night. I don't know who was with her, if one of her parents finally came and saw her shine.

I don't hear anything from her at all.

She starts going out with Greg. He doesn't speak to me either, keeps his arm firmly around Brianna when they are together, no flirting with anyone else, and I hear people say they are happy. That Brianna says Ryan is a loser and she's glad to be with a real guy, one who knows what he's doing.

Ryan grins when I tell him that, and then his smile fades.

"Sarah," he says, wrapping his arms around me, and even now, even when I miss Brianna so much, there's the thrill of being with him, of knowing that I can look at him without guilt, that I can touch him freely. That we are together.

"I don't care what she says," he says. "But you—do you care?"

"Not about you and me. But I . . . I miss her," I say, and he looks at me, his eyes intent. Focused only on me.

"I'm sorry," he says, and I know he is. I know he wishes things had ended between them in a way that hadn't brought me into it. I know he wishes he'd stayed and talked to me that first night, that summer night at the party. I know he wishes things had started differently for us, and I do too. But I'm not sorry I'm with him, and I wonder if Brianna knows that. If that's why she won't talk to me.

One afternoon, almost five months after the morning Brianna left my house without looking back, I tell Ryan I have to do something after school.

He kisses me, and for a second the world is perfect. I love that feeling. I love him.

But I still miss Brianna.

And so, after school, I go see her.

thirty-eight

When I get to her house, Brianna doesn't answer the door.

I know she's home though, because I see her car in the driveway and catch a glimpse of her hair as she passes by a window. It's as long and shiny as ever, dark and streaming out around her.

I look at the doorbell and then lean against it, think about how Brianna came over after Sam and the disaster of the dance. I'd told my parents I was fine, waved at them as they left to go shopping for new pantry shelves, and then lay dry-eyed on the sofa, ignoring everything, even Brianna when she showed up at the house and knocked on the door, calling my name.

I finally gave in and opened the door after she leaned against the doorbell, making it ring so many times I knew I'd dream about its stupid chime for days.

"I figured that would work," she'd said when I opened the door. "You know, I think whoever invented the doorbell was very angry at the world."

I'd laughed. Weakly, but still, it was a laugh, and Brianna had swept in, declaring my spot on the sofa "not nearly mopey enough." She'd buried me in pillows and blankets, bringing me food and lying on the floor in front of me with a plate perched on her head for crumbs, giggling as it slipped, and I'd forgotten everything that had happened for a while.

I know I can't do that for her now—Ryan isn't going away, and I don't want him to, don't wish for it and can't bring myself to pretend that I could—but I can be there for Brianna. I can try to make things right. I can say I'm sorry for what I left unsaid.

My fingers get numb after a while and I switch hands, try the doorbell with the rest of my fingers.

"Stop it!" Brianna yells through the door, and I grin like an idiot, so glad to hear her voice.

But I know her, and I don't let up on the doorbell, I wait for her to actually open the door.

I hear her sigh, then curse, and then the door flies open, showing Brianna standing in front of me, arms crossed over her chest and a furious look on her face.

"How retarded are you?" she says. "Did you come over here to get slapped again? Because I'd be happy to do that without you ringing the doorbell like an idiot."

"I'm sorry," I say, and she rolls her eyes at me and starts to shut the door.

"Brianna, wait," I say. "I know that's not enough, all right? But they're the only words I've got for how bad I feel. For the things I did. I should have told you I liked Ryan. I should have told you that . . ." I trail off, swallowing. Her face is so angry, and if I tell her that Ryan and I have a past that extends beyond the moment she saw us together, I might get slapped again for real.

"I should have told you that we . . . Brianna, we did more before you saw us together." I swallow again. "We kissed. Twice."

She doesn't hit me. She just stares at me, and then she laughs.

"You came over here to tell me that? Gee, Sarah, thanks. I'm so glad to know that not only did you steal my boyfriend and turn out to be a total slut, you were a lying slut before. That's great! Really, thanks so much, but the thing is, I've already figured out what a waste you are. Ryan will too, and when he does, you can bet I won't be crying over that."

She narrows her eyes. "Or is that why you're here? It's been, what, five months now? He's getting sick of you, right? I'm surprised he lasted this long. Sam couldn't even make it through one dance."

"I was wrong," I say quietly, ignoring the hurt and anger her words bring, the way she is trying to cut me down. "I should have been honest with you. I was just—Brianna, I was afraid you'd hate me."

"Well, you were right. Did you really think coming over here was going to work? That I'm just going to forget what you did to me?"

"It wasn't about you!" I say, and Brianna stills, the sneer on her face slipping, her expression shading into something different, something fearful and lost.

"I—I didn't do it to hurt you," I say. "I hated myself for how much I liked him. But I didn't—I didn't kiss him because he was your boyfriend. I didn't kiss him because I wanted to hurt you, although I know I did. I kissed him because I've liked him since eighth grade, Brianna. I know you know that. I know you remember that dance he asked me to."

"Oh, so now you're rewriting history?" she says, but her voice is shaking. "I'm the one who stole him, I'm the bad guy."

"No, that's not—I was wrong. I know that. But it wasn't—like I said, I didn't mean to hurt you. I didn't want to hurt you. I never meant to."

"Spare me," Brianna says, her voice going icy again, and I have said the wrong thing. It's true that I didn't mean to hurt her, that Ryan and I aren't about her, but she's heard it's not about her before, heard it from people who are supposed to love her, from her parents, who have never once put her first, never even put her in their hearts, and for all that I mean what I've said, I know all she will hear is betrayal.

"All right," I say softly. "I knew it would hurt you if you found out how I felt. I knew it was wrong to like him and I liked him anyway. I—I wanted him, Brianna. But how it all came out, that wasn't—I really did think you two were over. We both did. You have to believe me."

"No, I don't," Brianna says. "You did what you did, and now you've got what you wanted. You're with Ryan, but you're here, and I know how you feel. You're with someone who isn't totally there, who is with you but never really with you, and you know what? It won't change. Ryan will never love you. He couldn't even love me, so what chance do you have? He'll never even think about loving you, much less say it, and you threw away our friendship for . . ."

She trails off, taking a step back, shock on her face, and that's when I know I can still hurt her. That I am hurting her again. She knows me well enough to see what I have with Ryan. She sees what shines from my heart.

"He . . . he's told you?" she whispers. "He's said it? He loves you?"

"Brianna—"

"Oh," she says, her voice very quiet. "I didn't—" She looks down at the ground, blinking hard, and I know what this is costing her, I know that she hates to show herself like this, that hurt is something she's learned to hide and only reveals when it's so strong she can't hold it in. When it's all she feels.

"Brianna . . ." I say again, and then stop because there is nothing I can say to fix this. I can't make Ryan not love me.

And even if I could, I wouldn't, because I love him, I want to be with him, and I came to see Brianna because I miss her and I wish I hadn't hurt her. I wish I had handled things better.

But I don't unwish Ryan.

She looks at me then, and silence stretches between us. In the quiet I hear her swooping in to save me so long ago. I hear years of us talking and watching movies and working on homework. I hear us shopping and eating and just sitting together, silent in the way only friends can be, in the way you can talk without saying a word.

I hear us talking too, talking about her life, her parents. I remember holding her hand while she waited for neither of them to show up all the nights her plays started. All the nights she was someone else, all the nights she captured every crowd that came to see her plays, and they never once saw her. I hear and remember all the things that made our friendship.

I remember how she needed to be around my parents, my life. I remember how she knew I needed her to shine because it made me think that one day I might shine too.

I never thought it would be without her.

"You didn't tell him about Greg, did you?" she says, and it's not really a question. It's more like surprise.

I shake my head.

"I would have," she says. "I guess it makes you feel better, knowing that. Makes you think your 'sorry' is worth something. Makes you think you're better than me."

"No," I say. "It doesn't. And I'm not."

She looks at me again then, looks at me for a long time, and then shakes her head.

"I can't do it," she says. "I can't let you in again. Ryan was . . . that was one thing. He's just a guy. But you. Sarah, you were my best friend. You were the one person who was always—who I always knew would be there."

Don't be stupid. You need me.

"I'm still here," I say. "I just—Brianna, can't we be friends as who we really are? Can't I be who I am, can't I be just me?"

"Wait, you're really saying that? 'Can't I be who I am?' You mean, can I be friends with a liar, right? Is that what you're asking?"

I swallow. I look at her. I have lied. I've done stupid things. Awful things. I'm not perfect. But nobody is.

Not even her.

"Yes," I say. "That's what I'm asking," and she flushes, looking past me. She knows what I mean.

She knows, she has mistakes on her soul too, and I watch her pull herself together, watch her turn into the Brianna I've always thought belonged to the world but not to me. I watch her turn into the Brianna who looks at ease with everything. Who looks as if nothing and no one can ever surprise her, ever upset her. Ever truly reach her.

And then she shuts the door. No parting words, no goodbye, just her face, familiar and not, vanishing.

I don't wait to see if she'll come back. I know her—I do—and she won't. She will have walked away and she won't let herself look back.

I know she never will.

I drive home, thinking about what happened. About how sorry I am, but how it's not the sorry Brianna wants me to be. Our friendship was real, but it was built on me needing her, on me believing she made me someone, and I can't be that girl anymore.

I don't want to be that girl anymore.

I shouldn't have lied to her. I should have told her how I felt. I should have said, "I like Ryan," that first night, at that party before school started. I should have believed in what I felt. In myself.

I pull into my driveway. Ryan's car is there. I see him sitting on the porch, talking to my father. As I get out, my father waves, and Ryan smiles.

All the things I've thought about love are true. It's beautiful and terrible and it doesn't make things perfect. It ends things, and it brings beginnings.

This is mine.

ABOUT THE AUTHOR

Elizabeth Scott grew up in a town so small it didn't even have a post office, though it did boast an impressive cattle population. She's sold hardware, pantyhose, and had a memorable three-day stint in the dot-com industry, where she learned that she really didn't want a career burning CDs. She is also the author of *Bloom*; *Perfect You*; *Stealing Heaven*; *Living Dead Girl*; *Something, Maybe*; and *Love You Hate You Miss You*. She lives just outside Washington, D.C., with her husband; firmly believes you can never own too many books; and would love it if you visited her website, located at www.elizabethwrites.com.